The Iron Horse

Josiah Wakefield and Dan Sturgis are young civil war veterans, employed in the Territory of Nebraska by the Union Pacific Railroad to hunt down the hired gunmen who are wrecking their supply trains. As robbery is clearly not the motive, someone must be trying to slow up the railroad's westward progress.

After a vicious firefight on the trackless plains, their continued pursuit takes them to the dissolute city of Omaha where, in the company of their new acquaintance, Bill Hickok, they survive an ambush by paid assassins.

Their trouble is only just beginning, and they are to face deadly city marshal, Deke Pritchett, and the perils of being on board an Iron Horse, before a momentous finale. But just whose side is Bill Hickok really on?

By the same author

Blood on the Land
The Devil's Work

The Iron Horse

Paul Bedford

A Black Horse Western

ROBERT HALE · LONDON

ISBN 978-0-7198-1037-4

Robert Hale Limited
Clerkenwell House
Clerkenwell Green
London EC1R 0HT

www.halebooks.com

Typeset by
Derek Doyle & Associates, Shaw Heath
Printed and bound in Great Britain by
CPI Antony Rowe, Chippenham and Eastbourne

CHAPTER ONE

Spewing a great plume of black discharge from its towering smokestack, the monstrous contraption hove into view. It creaked and groaned and rattled as though possessing a tortured life of its own. Steam appeared to hiss and spit from every joint. Its frontage was adorned with a thrusting, lattice-worked iron prow. From the side this resembled a ram on a slaver's galley and was picturesquely known as a 'cow catcher'. The overall effect was sufficient to instil fear in any unsuspecting man or beast alike.

The huge 'Iron Horse' was new to Nebraska Territory in June 1866. In fact nothing like it had ever been seen on the Great Plains before, but its progress westward was relentless and unstoppable. A Cheyenne Indian had once tried to rope one with the intention of pulling it from the track, but it had jerked him from his pony and dragged him unmercifully. Unfortunately for Will Torrance, it was not merely bewildered tribesmen or a wandering herd of buffalo that was to cross paths with him. He had a far more dangerous foe awaiting him in the Platte River region that fine summer morning: his own countrymen.

About three miles beyond the settlement of Columbus, the gradient increased slightly. His fireman, Thaddeus

Spencer, heaved fresh wood into the voracious firebox. The heat and exertion caused fresh beads of sweat to form on that man's grimy forehead. They were hauling a lot of weight and couldn't afford to let the pressure drop. Behind them were flatbed carriages piled high with thirty-foot-long iron rails weighing six hundred pounds apiece, along with specially treated wooden crossties and vast containers of metal spikes.

Will's first intimation of trouble came when he happened to glance forward beyond the confines of the wooden cab and then off to his right. The land that stretched away before him was mostly flat and apparently limitless, but it was no longer empty. Six men sat upon motionless horses, their eyes intently fixed on the steam train's progress. The engine driver was a gregarious man and would normally have offered them a friendly wave. Yet these were not normal times. To his certain knowledge at least two supply trains had been derailed recently and there was something about the posture of the watching men that made him uneasy. They had not drawn their weapons, yet they did not have the look of casual spectators. The faces of the six were not concealed as one might expect from 'road agents', but that did not mean that their intentions were necessarily benign. Anxiety unexpectedly nibbled at his guts.

The track ahead curved away to the right, so that the heavily laden train would parallel the menacing horsemen. Dragging his eyes away from them, Will began to urgently scrutinize the rails that were to support the freight train's immense weight. Sure enough he was rewarded with a heart-stopping moment.

'Sweet Jesus, Thad,' he bellowed. 'They've lifted the rails!'

His fireman favoured him with a bewildered look. That man, enveloped by noise and smoke, had absolutely no idea who *they* were. Seizing hold of the huge brake lever, Will desperately heaved back on it. Despite the sound of tortured metal, he knew instinctively that he was too late. The vast locomotive was going to leave the track and would inevitably be followed by all the laden carriages. His eyes flitted briefly over to the waiting riders. They had not moved, no doubt wisely keeping well clear of the planned and expected destruction.

With the brakes locked on, sparks flew everywhere but it was all to no avail. The massive locomotive had noticeably slowed, but was a victim of its own weight and momentum. Will's eyes briefly locked with his companion's. In spite of the heat, the fireman's pallor had turned ashen. They both knew that survival was unlikely. Even as the front wheels left the rails, Thaddeus came to a desperate decision. Affectionately patting his companion on the shoulder, he abruptly turned and leapt from the left side of the highly polished cab.

The stricken machine ploughed into earth and grass at an unsupportable angle. Frantically clinging on to the brake lever, Will could only watch in helpless horror as the locomotive lurched to the right. His grasp broke free of the lever and he slammed bodily into the roof of the cab. Something snapped and he felt an agonizing pain in his left arm. With a truly stupendous din, the engine toppled on to its side and came to an abrupt halt. Will crashed down on to the side of the cab and lay there, temporarily winded and helpless. Chunks of wood from the tender were flying everywhere. A large piece struck his head a glancing blow and he suddenly tasted blood in his mouth. The flat bed carriages followed on as night follows day.

With a tremendous rending sound the vast consignment of rails, crossties and spikes broke free and tumbled over the prairie, just as had been intended.

Despite the intolerable pain in his arm, Will had worse things to contemplate. The firebox was open and some of its blazing contents had spilled out into the wooden cab. If he didn't clamber out, he could quite possibly burn to death. Gritting his teeth, he rolled over and somehow got to his feet. Unsteadily, he staggered into the gap between the cab and the now almost empty tender. Stumbling away from the wreckage, he had to veer off to avoid the top of the severed smokestack. There was a strange ringing in his head and he just could not possibly comprehend how the stack had arrived in that position.

The hissing of high-pressure steam and the noise from the settling cargo prevented him from hearing the approaching riders. It was only as he gazed round at the devastation that he noticed them. One of them took off at speed around the far side of the wrecked train. The others moved towards him at an unhurried pace. They surveyed the sight before them with apparent satisfaction.

The torment in Will's left arm prompted a wave of nausea to flow over him. Swaying from the effort, the Union Pacific employee attempted to gain a measure of relief by cradling it with his right hand. He just couldn't believe that anything could hurt so much.

'Looks like you're banged up some, mister.'

The strange voice possessed a harsh tone, utterly devoid of human compassion. Struggling to focus, Will peered over at him. He made no attempt to ask for help. Instead he merely stood his ground, swaying slightly, and waited on events. The single rider returned and offered a terse report. 'Neck's broke. He's buzzard bait.'

'That's too bad,' responded the earlier speaker flatly. 'Looks like you're all on your lonesome, railroad man.'

With that, he pulled out a Colt Army Revolver and drew back the hammer. Behind Will the cab had burst into flames, but he was completely oblivious to it. All he could see was the gaping muzzle aimed unwaveringly at his face. The gunman favoured him with an ominous grin and then, unbelievably, squeezed the trigger. The .44-calibre ball took him just above the bridge of his nose, flattened out some and then exited through the rear of his skull in a welter of blood and brain tissue. The momentum threw the engineer's now lifeless body back towards the locomotive that he had so lovingly maintained. His killer shrugged as he regarded the broken carcass before him, as though somehow disappointed at the ease of it all. Turning in his saddle, he addressed a skinny runt of a man.

'Rufus, pass me some of that bug juice you've got hidden away.'

'I ain't got any left, Jake,' whined that individual softly. His right eye twitched repeatedly as he parted with the lie.

As Jake's baleful glance settled on Rufus, he toyed with a skinning knife in his belt. 'You know I always need a drink after a kill. Hand it over or I'll open you up good.'

The other man swallowed nervously and reached into a saddle-bag. Jake got the drink that he so craved, but in doing so forgot one very important thing. As he and his gang of gun thugs rode off into Nebraska's trackless wastes, they left the telegraph line uncut. Such a mistake could cost a man dear!

CHAPTER TWO

The two riders approached the train wreck from the west. A blind man on a galloping horse could have found it. The remains of the burnt-out cab and tender were still smouldering, sending wisps of smoke up into the cloudless sky. The locomotive itself was still venting steam, like some great beast undergoing its death throes. It appeared strangely vulnerable, its condition emphasized by the fact that the bulbous smoke stack lay at an unnatural angle. The sickly sweet smell of burning flesh pervaded the site, but that hadn't deterred the local citizenry, who were busy looting the wreckage for anything useful. Some of them glanced nervously over at the new arrivals, trying to gauge their intentions. Those with a keen eye could not fail to see the array of weapons that they possessed.

Joe Wakefield ignored the scavengers; what happened to the cargo was not his problem.

'See if anyone survived that,' he remarked to his companion, before moving out to circle the scene.

It didn't take either of them long. Joe had just cut the trail as Dan rejoined him. The young man had lost some of his natural ebullience. His eyes were troubled as he made his report. 'Dead as a wagon tyre, engineer and fireman both. One with a broke neck, t'other with a ball in the head. They're both charred real bad from the fire. Those sons of bitches play rough.'

'From the look of these tracks there's six of them,' Joe replied. 'All on shod horses, so they sure ain't savages.'

'What are you aiming to do?'

'Pursue!'

'You right sure you really want to catch those fellers, Josiah?' Dan asked doubtfully. He came from a devout Christian family and never shortened his leader's name.

Easing his Sharps rifle out of its scabbard, Joe checked the seating of the percussion cap before turning to directly face Dan. 'This is the third attack on a Union Pacific train. Robbery's obviously not the motive. Colonel Cartwright gave me the job of finding out just what is, so how's it going to look if I turn tail first time out?'

His companion stared at him long and hard before finally emitting a resigned sigh. 'Just don't get us both kilt, Josiah. My mamma didn't raise me only to get shot dead.'

The plains stretched endlessly before them, but they weren't as flat and featureless as those back East thought. Undulations in the landscape were sufficient to hide those who chose to be hidden. There were also various rivers draining into the Platte. It was Joe Wakefield's belief that the wreckers would be overly confident and not expect pursuit, so they would probably make camp beside one and bide their time. Unlike Dan, he was not new to the role of manhunter. Having served in Hiram Berdan's Second Regiment of United States Sharpshooters during the recent Rebellion, he had an instinctive feel for tracking down and destroying the opposition. It was for that reason that he had been employed in his present role by the man charged with laying the Union Pacific Railroad's entire length of track. Shooting buffalo for the meat required to feed a huge workforce had enabled him to keep his eye in since the end of the conflict, but hunting 'big shaggies' didn't pay as well as hunting men.

The two men rode side by side in companionable silence for some while. They had known each other and been firm friends since early sixty-four. At twenty, Dan was the younger by four years and had only served in the Union Cavalry for the final year of the conflict. Youth and enthusiasm were there in abundance, but had been tempered by the harsh realities of warfare. So it was that he was able to hold his tongue and allow Joe to relentlessly survey the landscape, alert for the slightest disturbance. That man, matured far beyond his years by his experiences, would have been loath to admit it, but he felt a great affection for his good-natured companion. He looked upon him as the younger brother he had never had. However, none of this would have prevented him from putting them both in harm's way if the job required it. Josiah Wakefield possessed a certain icy cold-bloodedness, which was a necessary quality for a killer of men.

Time passed and so did the miles. Dan was assailed by hunger pangs and he belatedly realized that he had not eaten since he had breakfasted at the railhead. When Colonel Cartwright had been informed of the latest incident, he would tolerate no delay. Although no longer a serving officer, he still expected everything to be done at the double. Characteristically, he had demanded immediate and, if necessary, violent action. The colonel had assured Joe that all measures taken would be held to be within the law but Dan was not completely convinced. No longer sheltered by the military, he was concerned that he might one day have to face a man with a badge and a warrant in his hand. Sighing, Dan reached into a saddle-bag and extracted some strips of beef jerky. The dried meat was strongly smoked and tasted delicious. Leaning sideways in his McClellan saddle, he offered some to his companion.

'There'll be time for eating later,' Joe responded brusquely. 'We've done found them.'

Sure enough, some three hundred yards away, smoke was curling lazily up into the air from a camp-fire. Reining in, they rapidly dismounted. Whilst Dan ground-tethered the animals, Joe scrutinized the terrain before him through his drawtube spyglass. It was almost exactly as he had predicted. A river. A camp. Six men grouped around a fire. With hunger gnawing at him, Dan could almost smell the beans. Hell, they hadn't even mounted a guard.

Knowing that he had Dan to watch his back, Joe took the time to view each man in turn. The weapons that they carried would determine the course of action. He expected them to be well armed and they were, up to a point. All had revolvers. The four Spencers did not surprise him, but the two Henry Repeating Rifles gave them enviable firepower, so long as the copper rimfire cartridges did not expand with the heat of rapid discharge and cause a blockage. Yet none could match the long-range capability of his 'truthful' Sharps. The powerful breechloader boasted double-set triggers and a thirty-inch rifle barrel.

Dan hissed in his ear. 'What if it's not them, Josiah? What if they're just out hunting?'

'Then they're going to get one hell of a shock,' was the uncompromising reply. Relenting slightly, Joe turned to face him. 'Have you crossed any other tracks between here and the train wreck?'

'No,' Dan responded dubiously. 'But that don't mean there aren't any. It's a hell of a thing to kill a man, Josiah. I just want to be sure.'

'I am sure. Are you with me?'

The former cavalry trooper's features were twisted with indecision. He was painfully aware of his leader's eyes boring into him as he waited. Dan was beginning to realize that it was not always a good thing to work for a friend. Finally, silently, he nodded. That would have to do.

'All right, then. Chamber up that Spencer,' Joe commanded, returning his gaze to their prey. 'Ease off to the right and belly up to them. I'll let you get close in before I open fire. And remember, we need screamers. Don't kill them all!'

He did not see his young companion's reaction to that, but Joe knew that he sounded a lot more confident than he felt. What if it wasn't them?

Pushing the thought from his mind, he raised and adjusted the ladder sight on his Sharps rifle. Windage and elevation had to be taken into account. Three hundred yards was quite a long shot, but easily achieved when the target was a human torso. He had struck many an unsuspecting Confederate soldier at such range. Dan was crawling into position, so the sharpshooter had time to prepare. Placing a spare percussion cap in his mouth, he breathed slow and steady. Ideally, he would have preferred to lie down, but the ground before him was too uneven and would not have afforded him a shot. 'Dan had better not scare,' he reflected. 'They'll likely have us both if he does!'

Finally, it was time. Down on one knee, he thumbed back the hammer. Breathing steadily, Joe calmly sighted

14

down the long barrel. The group of six were obviously eating, because there was little movement. Lining up on a broad back, he squeezed the first trigger. 'God save me from misfires,' he muttered.

Just as his finger caressed the second trigger, a bearded face chanced to look up from the fire directly at him. What the gun thug saw or thought he saw mattered little. With a roar, the Sharps discharged. Ignoring the outcome, Joe half-cocked the hammer, depressed the under-lever and then blew into the breech. As someone bellowed out, 'Assassins!' he coolly loaded a linen cartridge, raised the falling block and then slipped on the copper cap from his mouth. Fully cocking the hammer, he again levelled the long gun. Only then did he finally observe the fall of shot.

All the men had dropped to the ground. At least one was hit and crying out in distress. The others loosed off a couple of wild shots in reaction. Joe remained on one knee, having chosen to ignore the 'fire and move' rule. The chances of them hitting him at that range were slim, and he surmised that they would soon be under fire from another source.

With divine timing, Dan opened up with his Spencer. As his weapon crashed out, hot ashes leapt up from the fire. Yelping with pain, one of the gang got on to all fours to scramble away. Squeezing off a well-judged shot, Joe then rapidly reached for another cartridge. The prairie wind whipped the powder smoke into his face and away. As ever he found the sulphurous whiff curiously exhilarating.

The .52-calibre ball had struck the unfortunate man in the hip, knocking him into the very fire from which he had been trying to escape. Howling in agony, he thrashed around, desperately trying to escape the flames that engulfed him. Completely ignoring him, his remaining companions hugged the ground and returned Dan's fire. Being the nearest, they erroneously considered him to be the most dangerous.

With his rifle reloaded, Joe leapt to his feet and advanced at a fast trot. Dan was in trouble. The fifteen-shot Henrys were peppering the ground around him, smothering any return fire that he might manage. What those rifles lacked in power, they made up for in speed. The sharpshooter was less than one hundred yards away before someone remembered his menacing presence. Shifting to meet the rapidly approaching threat, Rufus lined him up in his sights. In his eagerness to make a kill, the scrawny consumptive raised up from the ground.

With his chest heaving, Joe had no time for any considered marksmanship. Instinctively aiming low, he drew in a deep breath and fired on the up-roll. The large ball caught Rufus squarely in the chest and literally blew him backwards. Discarding the Sharps as though it was so much rubbish, Joe dragged his Colt Army from its military-issue flap holster and charged at the campsite, screaming foul blasphemies. A red mist had enveloped him. His blood was up. Nothing else could account for such a suicidal display. He cocked and fired three times. The .44-calibre balls from the single-action revolver failed to strike flesh, but they disrupted any return fire. A vicious-looking thug in a flash waistcoat clambered to his feet, chambering a cartridge into his Henry Rifle. As Joe juddered to a halt, a bullet from Dan's Spencer lifted the top of the man's head clean off. Blood and brain matter cascaded over the dead man as he crumpled to the ground.

The Union Pacific needed prisoners, and only one man remained unblooded. Yet, although armed with both a belt gun and a Spencer, he no longer wanted any part of the conflict. Turning rapidly away, he began to 'tote the mail' for the river. Dan wasn't near enough to intercept him and Joe had had a belly full of running.

'One chance,' he bellowed. 'Stop or I fire!'

The river bank beckoned and the runaway increased speed. Cursing, Joe took a two-handed grip and levelled his revolver. Feeling no guilt whatsoever at shooting a man in the back, he squeezed the trigger. The soft lead ball caught the fugitive between the shoulder blades and neatly pitched him into the river. No longer any kind of threat, he could keep. With two chambers remaining, Joe again cocked his piece and turned back to the camp. Bloody carnage along with the dreadful smell of burning flesh awaited him. Only one man still lived, and Dan had a tale to tell.

'Sweet Jesus, Josiah. I ain't never seen the like! Your first shot took two of them down. I saw it all. It went straight through the first feller and hit this son of a bitch in the shoulder. Hot dang!'

Joe realized that such marksmanship could be perceived as quite an achievement, but all he felt was a strange emptiness inside and an unsettling weakness in his legs. He had taken part in numerous skirmishes during the war to preserve the Union, but that had seemed different somehow. Back then he had been in uniform, surrounded by his comrades and under orders.

The protests of the wounded man dragged him back to the present. 'You pus weasels have got no call to treat me like this. I've done nothing wrong.'

'You call wrecking a train nothing, mister?' Dan's indignation was genuine. The sight of the two burnt corpses back at the track had stayed with him.

'We didn't have anything to do with that,' retorted Jake

indignantly. 'We just happened upon it when it was all over.'

The leader and sole survivor of the gang was an odious-looking individual with a pock-marked face and rank, greasy hair, but he possessed a certain native cunning. Observing his two captors carefully, he tried to assess his chances. Believing that familiarity was his best bet, he tried another tack. 'Say, you fellers wouldn't happen to have some "Oh Be Joyful" on you, would you? This wound's given me a powerful thirst.'

Joe had had enough. Ramming his gun muzzle into the side of Jake's head, he rasped out, 'Land sakes, I tire of this. Tell me who you work for now, or you'll take a lead pill.'

The other man's attempt at bonhomie abruptly disappeared. 'Go to hell!'

'After this day's work I believe that I shall,' Joe replied in all seriousness. The reality of being a back-shooter as well as a sharpshooter had just sunk in and it didn't sit well with him. He had been pushed into it by the activities of the piece of scum in front of him and he could feel anger beginning to build within him. Holstering his revolver, he reached down and picked up one of the Henry Repeaters. Turning it over in his hands, he immediately noticed something strange about it, but that could wait. Steeling himself, he placed the muzzle over his prisoner's shoulder wound.

'If you don't tell me who you work for and where I can find him, I'll have to hurt you bad.'

A queasy look came over Jake's face. 'If I tell you anything, I'm dead anyway.'

'Josiah, perhaps we should. . . .' Dan's fresh face was clouded with concern. As it happened, his companion didn't like what was about to take place any more than he did. He just didn't show it.

Apparently relenting slightly Joe said, 'Just tell us where in Columbus you get your instructions. Then we'll patch you up and set you on your horse.'

Then, without warning, he leaned on the butt of the rifle. Jake's high-pitched scream made both railroad men flinch. Blood coated the gun muzzle. Joe felt sick to his stomach, whilst his young companion swiftly averted his eyes.

'Omaha,' howled out their captive. 'We met him in the ma—'

Jake's head exploded like a ripe melon. His blood and brain matter splashed everywhere. Only then did they hear the gunshot. Both men dropped to the ground, with Joe reaching for his spyglass. Some four hundred yards away, a man in a duster coat had mounted his horse and was urging it to speed. Without his rifle, the former Berdan sharpshooter had no chance of hitting the runaway, and quite probably little chance with it. The accuracy had been breathtaking.

CHAPTER THREE

'*Omaha!*'

Thomas Cartwright's teeth, almost lost under his luxurious beard, worked ferociously on a fat cigar butt. His sunburnt forehead creased under the effort of intense thought. Thirty-four years old, he had been a lieutenant colonel in the war and was now charged with building a railroad. He was five feet eight inches of belligerent muscle and not a man to trifle with.

'Omaha is a railroad town,' he remarked fiercely. 'It was just a few shacks before the Union Pacific rolled in. You're telling me that those bull turds were working out of our town?'

'I don't reckon that feller was lying, Mister Cartwright,' Joe replied soberly. 'He was in an awful lot of pain at the time.'

The railhead boss regarded him pensively. 'Six men, all dead, you say.'

'That's how it ended up, Mister Cartwright. It wasn't my choosing, but the odds were stacked too high to go in easy.'

'Yeah, well, I guess you did good, Wakefield.' As he uttered that grudging praise, the 'track boss's' expression was hard to read. It contained surprise, for sure, but also something more intangible that made Joe wonder whether he and Dan had actually done the right thing in tackling the wreckers. Possibly aware that his remark had fallen short of outright praise, Cartwright continued with, 'Those responsible have got to learn that they can't just ride roughshod over an operation as big as this.'

As if to support that statement there came an unremitting stream of profanity uttered in a strong Irish accent as Shaughnessey, the 'walking boss', strode past the plush carriage containing the three men. That forceful individual drove on the gangs of sweating workers as they lowered the iron rails on to the waiting crossties and spiked them down. Four rails were laid each minute, hour after hour. Thanks to their unceasing toil, the railhead was rapidly approaching the small settlement of Grand Island, near the north bank of the Platte River. Everything was carried out with military precision, which was not surprising as the construction of the Union Pacific was in the hands of ex-officers from the victorious North's rapidly contracting army.

'Something's not right about any of this,' Cartwright continued thoughtfully. 'Three derailments without robbery or demands. And then there's the killings. It's almost as though the bastards are trying to scare us into stopping the supply trains. One thing's for sure, it's slowing us up. The terrain's flat, so the grading proceeds swiftly, but without more rails the track-laying won't be able to keep pace. Without track we can't make any money and without that we can't fund all this.'

He stopped long enough to light the well-gnawed cigar, apparently oblivious to the oppressively hot atmosphere in the carriage. As it began to emit clouds of pungent smoke, he seemed to come to a decision. 'You two are going to take a train ride. There's at least one returning for supplies tomorrow. If the man *or men* behind that gang are in Omaha, then that's where you need to be. And you might could see your way to hiring some more help. You're likely going to need it.'

Dan was aghast. 'What if *our* train gets derailed, sir?'

Cartwright slowly shook his head in despair. 'Son, they're not going to wreck it heading east. It'll be empty!'

The young man flushed with embarrassment. To shift attention from him, Joe proffered one of the rifles that they had recovered. 'What about this?'

The former colonel knew his weapons. '*This* is a Winchester. Similar to the Henry, but a whole lot better. The loading gate in the side of the frame makes for fast reloading, even lying down. With the wooden forestock, you won't burn your poor little hand when the barrel heats up. It's so new I haven't even seen one out West before.'

'What shall I do with it?'

'You killed a man for that gun, Wakefield. I surely ain't going to try and take it off you.'

When the Union Pacific Railroad heading west on a diet of whiskey met the Central Pacific Railroad heading east on a diet of tea, the journey time from coast to coast would be reduced from six months to a mere six days. The entire span of the recently unified United States of America would be irrevocably linked for the first time. What the telegraph had achieved for communication, the railroad would achieve for transport. The steam locomotive was a modern miracle, but in its current state it was also a very basic and uncomfortable form of travel. Wood burners emitted vast quantities of glowing sparks, which had to be controlled by a cone-shaped deflector under the mouth of the chimney and a wire screen covering the exit. These measures could never completely stop flying sparks from blowing back on the travellers, yet to close the rudimentary windows meant suffering in the stifling summer heat.

The two men were sitting on hard-backed wooden seats in the single passenger carriage that formed part of the train. Its other components were all flat cars, designed to carry track-laying materials. The only other passengers were three sullen tracklayers, discharged by the walking boss for persistently tardy work. They had been offered one-way tickets from the railhead near Grand Island to the supply depots in Omaha. Generosity didn't come into it. The railroad just wanted rid of them. They sprawled untidily over the bench seats, happy to rest from their eternal toil, but resentful at their abrupt dismissal. The one-hundred-and-fifty-mile journey would take some five hours, including a stop at Columbus.

With plenty of time to think, Dan had obviously got something gnawing at him. 'Why didn't you tell the colonel about the seventh man?'

Joe regarded his friend pensively. 'I don't really know. Maybe because it could have made us look sloppy. And it certainly wouldn't have changed anything. All that ass boil wants is results. He's cross-grained by nature and not interested in anything unless it directly affects his precious railhead.'

With that he fell contemplatively silent. The real issue was just what someone stood to gain by slowing up the advance of the Iron Horse. Could it be that the Central Pacific was trying to steal a march on their rivals? The more track that they laid, the more they stood to gain in government grants. Wrecking and outright murder seemed a bit excessive, though, even in such a ruthless environment.

Such thoughts occupied Joe Wakefield for some time until, gazing out of the window, he realized that they were again approaching Columbus. The stricken locomotive was still lying on its side. In the past twenty-four hours, the good townsfolk had seized anything that they could carry and the track had been hastily repaired. A few minutes later, the eastbound supply train approached the rough-cut buildings that made up the settlement. It was here that the two men encountered an individual the like of which they had never seen before.

The locomotive stopped next to an elevated water tank. As Joe stood up to stretch, a tall character wearing city clothes took his attention. The man's walk was slow, yet deliberate, as he moved towards the single carriage. There was a panther-like grace to his bearing. Long, curly golden hair splayed out over the collar of his frock coat. A luxuriant moustache adorned his somewhat ill-formed upper lip. Two Colt Navy Sixes were tucked, butts facing forward, into holsters on his highly polished leather belt. As he was about to mount the first step, the stranger's eyes flicked over to take in Joe's curious gaze. There was an intensity about them that gave him pause. And that wasn't his only concern.

As the new arrival temporarily moved out of sight, Joe dropped back down next to his friend. 'Take a look at the city gent coming in, *and* at what he's carrying.'

Dan had plenty of opportunity to do just that; such was the man's leisurely progress down the central aisle. Just prior to him reaching their position, a brawny tracklayer happened to clamber across from the far side of the carriage and dropped down on to the seat opposite.

24

Someone or something outside had clearly taken his interest.

'Golden Hair' came to a halt next to their section. Although slimly built, there was an aura of power about him that hinted at hidden capabilities. Having favoured the two manhunters with a mild glance, his eyes glittered as he viewed their new neighbour. 'You're sitting in my seat,' he stated softly.

The Union Pacific employee had shoulders like house sides and hands like hams. He could doubtless lift or hammer anything that was required of him. Having been recently made unemployed, he was also in just the right mood for a fight. Gazing sharply up at the interloper, he laughed out loud before replying, 'And you're a black liar, mister!'

With that, he got to his feet and stood waiting, confident that his mere appearance would be sufficient to back up such strong words. Lifting his powerful arms, he began to flex his fingers, as though inviting a response. As the other man was within range of his fists, he was clearly not worried about the highly visible belt guns. Knowing that most confrontations usually fizzled out, Joe fully expected more wordplay from one party or the other before they drifted apart, but it was not to be.

The sudden violence occurred with lightning speed. Golden Hair threw the linen duster coat that he was clutching in his left hand in a roundhouse swipe that lashed into the labourer's head. Caught unawares, that individual attempted to fend it off, and in doing so left himself open to a vicious blow on the forehead from the butt of a Colt Navy Revolver. With a groan, he crumpled to the floor of the railway carriage.

His assailant deftly twirled his weapon, so that the

seven-and-a-half-inch octagonal barrel was suddenly pointing in the general direction of anyone who might choose to intervene. Tossing the coat on to his intended seat, he condescendingly drawled, 'Either of you track hands want to make more of this?'

Apparently neither of them did, because they both kept their places. Either of them would have happily indulged in a fistfight, but there was little point in getting shot dead attempting to claim a window seat. Nodding slowly, Golden Hair slipped the revolver back into its resting place and turned to face his new neighbours. An easy smile crept over his features as he addressed them. 'I take it you gentlemen have no objection to *my* sitting here?'

Although intrigued by their new acquaintance, Joe did not intend that the man should deal out any more hard knocks. 'I doubt if that Navy Six could withstand another blow like that,' he remarked mildly. 'And if I did object, it wouldn't be my fists that I'd use on you.'

The interloper's smile froze. 'Oh, and what would you employ?'

Joe silently gestured towards the side of the carriage, where he had placed his Sharps.

A guarded look replaced the smile. 'Long distance, eh. That might could make you a hunter of sorts. What particular critters do you favour?'

'Two legs or four. Makes no difference to me. What's your weapon of choice?'

Golden Hair gently patted his brace of Colts as he replied, 'These answer tolerably well across a Faro table.'

With that, he turned sideways across the bench seat, tilted his wide-brimmed hat over his face and lowered his head on to the duster coat that had so taken Joe's attention. Their discourse was obviously at an end.

His two hosts regarded each other briefly and shrugged. Whether asleep or not, the newcomer's presence had affected their ability to speak freely. They were left with little choice other than to submit to the monotonous sounds on board the train and doze fitfully.

Some three hours later Golden Hair began to stir. The vanquished tracklayer had long before staggered off to nurse a headache, retribution apparently far from his mind. They were closing on the territorial capital: Omaha. Joe decided that it was time to voice a decision that he had just come to. Using his boot to gently nudge the other man, he remarked, 'If you would oblige me, sir, I would have words with you before we arrive.'

For a man who had supposedly been slumbering soundly, that man's gaze was remarkably keen as it focused on the speaker. 'Talk away, friend. I always welcome a parley.'

'We work for the railroad,' began Joe, careful to keep his voice low. 'But not as surveyors or tracklayers or some such. We're more like trouble-shooters. And believe me, sir, there is a shit load of trouble in these parts. So I'm looking to hire on men that can handle themselves. Men like you.'

'How do you know that you can trust me?'

'I don't, but I'd rather have you with me than against me. Five dollars a day and found. What do you say to that?'

'What makes you think I might be against you?'

Joe's answer was deliberately evasive. 'Those duster coats turn up in the strangest places. Been meaning to get myself one for a while now.'

Golden Hair stared at him long and hard. His brown eyes were like flints. Then finally he spoke. 'I believe I like

27

you. Given loose rein I could imagine working for you for a while. You've got yourself a new top hand.'

Favouring him with a broad smile, Joe announced, 'I'm Joe Wakefield from Wayne County, Pennsylvania. This is Dan Sturgis. What name do you go by?'

At that moment the train jerked violently, as it slowed on its approach to the engine sheds in Omaha. Taken by surprise, Joe lurched forward. As though seeking to steady him, his new employee grabbed his hand in a vicelike grip that he struggled to match. 'The name's Hickok,' he replied. 'James Butler Hickok. My friends call me Bill.'

CHAPTER FOUR

The sun was beginning to set as they clambered down from the railway carriage. Before them lay a mainly wooden city, brimming over with vice and degradation. Barely twelve years old, it owed its existence to land speculators across the water in neighbouring Council Bluffs. Its continued expansion was due to both its position on the Missouri River and the fortuitous arrival of the Union Pacific Railroad. It had become a base of operations for that gigantic enterprise, with continuous steamboat traffic delivering the greedily consumed raw materials.

As only an infrequent visitor, Joe really should have been observing his surroundings, but instead his mind was struggling to recall where he had heard the name 'Hickok' before. In a huge and expanding country, containing vast open spaces, the delivery of news was erratic at best. Many men attracted a reputation, often for the wrong reasons. The question was, had he made the right decision in hiring him?

The projectile smashed into Dan's left shoulder, its momentum carrying him back into the ubiquitous mud. Another one clipped the heel of Joe's right boot, almost pitching him forward into the same substance. Taken

29

unawares and totally unprepared, agonizing bloody death seemed to be the only outcome. Then Bill Hickok opened up with his Colts. Struggling desperately to catch his balance, Joe heard rather than saw the rapid gunshots. Leaving his saddle-bags where they lay, he retained the Sharps and crouched down next to Dan. Blood welled up through the material of his stricken friend's jacket. Tears of pain streamed from anguished eyes as the young man attempted to move. Hooking an arm under his right shoulder, Joe heaved him to his feet.

'The cockchafers are using the first floor of the hotel,' bellowed Hickok. 'Get your possum on to the boardwalk and follow me.'

With that, he fired another ball at the Cozzens House Hotel and then ran full chisel for the main entrance. Depositing Dan out of harm's way as instructed, Joe remained with him just long enough to stuff his kerchief over the shoulder wound before hobbling over to join his new employee. Meeting him at the entrance to the gaudy establishment, he cocked his buffalo gun. Hickok had a revolver in each hand and appeared to be calm, collected and completely in his element.

'You line that cannon up on the stairs,' he commanded. 'Anything moves, pop a cap!'

With that, the flamboyant shootist burst into the lobby, scouring the room for any potential threat. Not surprisingly, the large space was suddenly empty of any residents. Joe peered down open sights with a feverish intensity, all the while praying that the ambuscade did not include a back-shooter. From the first floor there came the sound of a woman crying out in pain. That just had to be connected.

Hickok motioned for his new boss to shift position to

the foot of the stairs. As Joe complied, he then rushed for the half-landing. So far neither of them had caught a glimpse of their two assailants, but that was about to change.

In response to Hickok's approach, a rifle swung into view, its muzzle aimed directly at his chest. Instinctively, Joe drew a bead on the bearded thug behind it and fired. In the close confines of the lobby, the discharge sounded like an artillery piece. Shrouded in black powder smoke with his ears ringing, he had no idea who or what he might have hit. Then the screaming started. 'I'm dying, Wes. The bastard's kilt me!'

On the half-landing, Hickok fired once for effect, and then bounded up to the first floor. Confident that he was covered, Joe followed at a slower pace, reloading as he climbed.

'Reckon you just saved my life, Mister Wakefield,' drawled the pistoleer. 'That's a real crowd-pleaser you've got there.'

Before them, in an ever-expanding pool of blood, lay the first assassin. He was a burly, hairy fellow with red froth now flowing over his whiskers. The heavy ball had entered him in the gut at a steep angle. With the soft lead flattening on impact, it had no doubt blown a sizeable hole through his back. He was wailing with the pain and would be a while dying, but was no longer a threat. His Winchester lay where it had fallen, a duplicate of the one that Thomas Cartwright had been holding in his hands the previous day. Joe kicked it out of possible reach and then removed a six-shooter from the expiring man's belt.

'This sack of shit's finished,' he remarked laconically. 'What else have we got up here?'

Together, he and Hickok surveyed the hotel landing.

With no natural light, it was illuminated by a selection of flickering oil lamps. There were five closed doors on either side.

'Not a joyful prospect,' Hickok muttered, 'checking every one for another long gun.'

The agonized keening of his victim was playing on Joe's nerves, so he limped quietly down the corridor. Stopping between two doors, he stood and listened. He didn't have long to wait. From one of the bedrooms came a plaintive whimper. It could only be fear or pain from the same woman as before.

As Hickok joined him, Joe whispered, 'I need him *alive* if possible.'

If the other man heard that, he didn't trouble to acknowledge it. Instead he reached out and tapped on the door with the muzzle of one Colt. 'Knock, knock,' he playfully announced.

With a tremendous splintering crack, a bullet tore through the timber. Hickok kicked hard at the door and then stepped sharply back. Under such force, the wood around the lock splintered and it swung open.

A woman screamed out, 'Don't shoot. For pity's sake don't shoot!'

Poking his Sharps around the doorframe, Joe risked a quick glance. Across the room, with their backs to the window, stood two people. Wes turned out to be a cadaverous individual, so slight of build that he was almost completely hidden by his human shield. She was quite obviously a Dutch gal: a woman of easy virtue. Tight-fitting, gaudy clothes and too much rouge said it all. Sadly for her she was not at her best. With her left arm brutally twisted behind her back, streaming tears had ruined her make-up.

'Anyone pops a cap on me and it's the fast trick that takes it,' spat Wes venomously.

As Joe replied, he was conscious of his companion taking careful aim from across the entrance. 'If I fire this piece at close range, it'll punch straight through her and into you. Is that what you want, Wes?'

Such action would have required a callous disregard for human life, the like of which he did not possess. Yet Wes could not know that, because he quite obviously had no such qualms. As a consequence his clammy features suddenly registered gut-churning fear.

'It doesn't have to be like this, Wes,' he continued softly. 'Just lower your piece and you have my word that you'll live.'

His weapon began to waver. A Winchester is too heavy to aim with one hand for long. Indecision began to take hold and Joe knew then that he had him.

Hickok's Navy Six discharged with a painful roar. The ball struck Wes's top lip, taking several teeth with it. The momentum was sufficient to carry him into and out of the window directly behind him. Showered with blood and grey matter, the woman screamed with horror, but at least she still lived. Death had robbed Wes of his vice-like grip on her wrist; otherwise she too would have been lying in the street covered with broken glass.

'I'll leave you to wish him well on his journey,' remarked Hickok drolly. 'I always need a shot of Old Red Eye after a kill.'

Peering out of the window, Joe Wakefield noticed that nobody seemed overly concerned at the turn of events. If there was any law in Omaha that day, it sure wasn't in any all-fired hurry to show itself.

CHAPTER FIVE

'Reckon I earned my first day's pay, Mister Wakefield!'

James Butler Hickok sat, apparently completely at ease, with his back to the wall in a saloon on 9th Street. He sipped house whiskey from a short glass and showed every sign of enjoying it whereas, after that day's events, black coffee was all Joe could manage. Physically, he had escaped with nothing worse than a sore heel. What really rankled was the damage to his only pair of boots, and of course his friend's injury. Dan was asleep in a hotel room, having been liberally dosed with laudanum by the local sawbones. Extracting the ball had been easy; the small pieces of clothing less so. Although he had only suffered a flesh wound, there was always the danger of greenrod setting in if the injury became infected.

'I'd take it kindly if you'd call me either Joe or Josiah,' that man replied. '*Mister Wakefield* has me looking for the warrant in your hand.'

'Then let it be Joe,' responded Hickok immediately. 'Josiah sounds altogether too biblical and I was never one for the scriptures. For myself, I prefer to be called Bill by my friends. It sounds less formal.'

Joe favoured him with a broad smile. He was developing

34

a genuine liking for the man, yet he told himself to remain circumspect. There was something more than the mere possession of a duster coat troubling him and he could not contain it any longer. 'There is something I would know. I asked you to take that murderous scoundrel alive, yet you completely ignored me. Why?'

Bill regarded him steadily and unblinkingly as he replied. 'For the best of all reasons. Survival. That pus weasel's hand was trembling like a bitch on heat. Like enough he'd have triggered that rifle without proposing to.'

His explanation carried weight. It indicated experience and practicality in equal measure. Anyway, there was little point in disputing it and creating ill feeling, because right then Joe needed all the help that he could get. Nodding slowly, he took a sip of coffee and left the matter there. A companionable silence settled over them as they imbibed, only to be broken by the advent of a most unsettling thought.

'It occurs to me,' Joe remarked quietly, 'that nobody in this city should have known in advance of our arrival or the business that brought me here. Those two assassins had to have been forewarned by telegraph.'

Keeping his voice low, Bill leaned forward and increased the stakes. 'Which gives you the man that sent you here, along with anyone that chanced to overhear and, of course, the telegraph operator.'

Joe found it hard to believe that Colonel Cartwright could be behind such a murderous plot. The man lived and breathed the railroad. Someone else had to be involved. There was only one place to start.

'Come morning we must visit the telegraph office. Any message had to be both sent and received by an operator.'

Bill momentarily toyed with his shot glass, as though weighing something up. 'Are you right sure you want to follow this trail? You survived today because they didn't expect backup, which must now make me a marked man as well.'

Joe was beginning to regret not having brought along his newly acquired Winchester. Not that it mattered. Dan wouldn't be firing his, or indeed anything else two-handed for a while. As for Hickok's inquiry, that made him the second employee to question his course of action in recent days.

'I took on a job and I mean to see it through, Bill. If that doesn't sit well, then you can collect your day's pay and depart with no hard feelings.'

The pistol fighter regarded him solemnly for a few seconds, before favouring him with an apparently genuine smile. 'I reckon I'll stick around. You can use the help and I can use the specie. But if you're going to stay with this kind of work you'd do well to cut the flap off that holster. You're not in the army any more and the enemy's not wearing butternut grey and firing muzzleloaders. The time it takes to palm that pistola will see you paroled to Jesus!'

The next morning, as they breakfasted on pancakes and coffee, Joe Wakefield and Bill Hickok received a singularly hostile visitor. The big man observed them briefly from the threshold of the busy eating house, before directly approaching them. He was of above average height and broad-shouldered, wore a sombre black frock coat and sported a city marshal's badge. No weapon was visible, but the noticeable bulge under his left arm suggested a shoulder rig. As is sometimes the way, Joe took an immediate dislike to the newcomer before the man had even opened his mouth. What followed only confirmed that feeling.

'You boys must be the railroad detectives that bust up my town yesterday.'

As it appeared to be a statement rather than a question, the two men continued with their repast. Showing no emotion at their snub, the marshal pulled up another chair and twirled it back to front, before straddling it with his arms leaning on the backrest. From that position, he scrutinized them closely, all the while chewing remorselessly on a cheek full of tobacco. It didn't go unnoticed by either of the railroad men that his holdout weapon was within easy reach.

'Yeah, I've decided,' he remarked menacingly. 'I really don't like you two!'

Bill regarded the lawman mildly before offering him some coffee.

'I'll stick with my plug,' came the cold response. 'In the meantime I want to know just what you two snake-eyed sons of bitches are doing here.'

For the first time, Joe stopped eating and faced him directly. The marshal was a nasty-looking cuss with close-set eyes and a drooping black moustache. There was a hard set to his jaw and a meanness to his mouth that suggested he very probably didn't run a friendly jail. Knowing that the Union Pacific carried plenty of weight in those parts, Joe decided to push back.

'And where were you when my friend and I came under deadly fire from the hotel? If it wasn't for my breakfast guest here, we'd both be mustered out.'

On the point of replying, the marshal suddenly twisted round on his chair and with remarkable accuracy sent a revolting stream of black juice into the nearest spittoon.

When he turned back, his face held a dangerous touch of colour. Fixing his cold eyes on Joe's new employee, he asked, 'Are you his heel hound, then?'

That man stiffened and then shifted in his seat. His eyes became chips of ice. When he replied, his voice had an ominous tone to it. 'The name's Hickok, Marshal. Bill Hickok. Just what is it about us that happens to offend you?'

'Hickok,' came the scornful reply, 'I've heard of you. You're supposed to be some kind of fearsome pistol fighter. Well you don't impress me with that two-gun rig!'

'Have you got any papers on me?'

'I've got plenty that could match up to a lily-livered back-shooter!'

It was at that point that both men realized that the marshal had to have backup. His right hand lingered near his shoulder rig and with such outrageous insults, he was definitely on the prod. Therefore, there had to be someone else supporting his play *and* acting as a witness, in case any gunplay had to be justified before a judge.

Joe very slowly brought both hands up on to the table. After a short and highly charged delay, Bill followed suit. If there were going to be any shooting, then the lawman would have to instigate it. Only then did Joe say his piece.

'If there's going to be any kind of ruckus, then *you'll* have to start it. We're just here to eat. If somebody wants damages for yesterday's shindig, tell them to put a claim in to the Union Pacific. You carry messages, don't you, law dog?'

The marshal flinched as though he had been struck. Incandescent rage flared on his features and he gripped the chair back until his knuckles showed white. Joe truly believed that he had pushed too hard. With an obvious effort, the 'law dog' retained just enough self-control to form a response.

'Yeah, I carry messages and I've one to give you. And it brings me to the which of why I'm here. I don't like the goddamned railroad. This was my town until they came sashaying in here with their big-city money and their grand plans for *our* future. I don't care who you two fellers work for. If you step out of line in my town I'll lock you up and throw away the key. Ask anybody about Marshal Deke Pritchett and they'll tell you to step wide of him.'

With that, he stood up, thrust the chair away and strode out of the eating house without a backward glance. Only then did a burly plug-ugly hefting a massive Colt Dragoon rise up and follow him out.

Bill met Joe's glance and raised his eyebrows as he commented sardonically, 'Looks like you've been warned, Joe Wakefield.'

The office of the Pacific Telegraph Company was only a short walk away but, after their recent encounter, they proceeded with great care. Keeping to the boardwalk, they avoided open spaces and maintained a safe distance between each other. It appeared that they were up against not only railroad saboteurs but the local law as well. Or perhaps they were one and the same. It loomed large in Joe's mind that Jake's last word on Earth had begun with the letters 'm-a'. Could that possibly mean the marshal's office? Such thoughts did not sit well with him. With Dan temporarily incapacitated and Bill Hickok a relatively unknown quantity, he felt as though he were between a rock and a hard place.

The two men reached the telegraph office without incident. There were plenty of people on the muddy street that morning, but none that appeared overtly threatening. Some unfortunates were not even able-bodied. Two invalids passing the time of day outside of their destination were quite pitiful to behold. Aged far beyond their years, both were wearing remnants of Union Blue and both were amputees. One had lost his entire right leg, the other his lower left arm. Their expressions were blank, their eyes devoid of hope. They were bitter proof that although the actual fighting had ended, the Civil War would live on for a long time to come. One of the broken veterans glanced up at the tall, well-made young man and muttered, 'You won't get no change out of that miserable bastard in there.' Then he cackled mirthlessly and went back to people-watching.

Joe was well aware that, but for the grace of God, he could easily have been in a similar condition. Tearing his gaze from them, he entered the office. By pre-arrangement, Bill was to remain outside on guard. The Pacific Telegraph Company ran the communication link between Omaha and Salt Lake City in Utah. Any message from the railhead had to have come in on their wire. Joe approached the counter and took in the somewhat officious-appearing individual before him. The clerk had the soft, puffy flesh of a man who spent his entire life indoors. He had access to the magical machine: the telegraph key and relay system. It allowed him an exaggerated sense of power, which he no doubt exercised to the full over those timid enough to allow it.

'I couldn't possibly divulge any information about messages received in this office,' the clerk huffily replied, in answer to Joe's inquiry. His manner suggested that his office enjoyed a similar sanctity to that of a church.

Joe tried again. 'I am directly employed by *Colonel*

Cartwright of the Union Pacific. I have the right to inspect any messages relating to railroad business.'

'I don't care if you're employed by General U. S. Grant himself; unless a message is for you and you *pay* for it, I can't help you. Or rather, I *won't* help you.' The young man seemed to derive great satisfaction from that final sentence.

Joe could feel a familiar anger building up within him, but he retained control for the present. The particular emphasis on one word had given him an idea. Carefully leaning his long rifle against the counter, he then reached into an inner pocket of his jacket. With a flourish, he extracted an object that was sure to generate great interest.

The night before Joe had left home to join the Union forces, his father had proudly presented him with a large, privately minted Californian gold piece. It was a treasured possession that had supposedly been obtained during his travels, following service in the Mexican War. By some miracle he had managed to avoid spending it. Wakefield Senior had never clearly explained just how he had got his hands on it, which somehow only seemed to add to its allure. The valuable metal was intended as a bargaining tool of last resort, to assist with young Wakefield's survival if all else failed.

As the infinitely desirable gold piece appeared on the counter, a sea change came over the clerk. His eyes, already accentuated by a pair of bottle-bottomed glasses, widened to ridiculous proportions as he regarded it with awe. He began to lick a pair of slug-like lips. The supercilious manner had fallen away like a discarded coat.

Joe placed the forefinger of his left hand on the precious object, pinning it to the counter. 'Take a closer look,' he suggested.

The only way for the Pacific Telegraph employee to do that was to lean forward, exactly as Joe had intended. As the man innocently lowered his head towards the counter, Joe's right hand snaked round behind it. Grabbing hold of the unresisting skull, he exerted all his considerable strength and slammed it on to the polished wooden surface. The resulting crunch was enough to make a statue cringe. Despite the agony of a broken nose and possibly some teeth, his victim was too stunned to cry out. Blood and snot cascaded from his mangled snout as he staggered back. Tears streamed from behind his damaged spectacles as he tried to understand what had just happened.

'You've broken my *do*se,' he wailed through mashed lips.

Totally indifferent to his suffering, Joe then did two things simultaneously. He tucked the gold piece safely back into his jacket and drew his revolver.

'That's going to be the least of your worries,' he snarled.

Some few minutes later, the railroad detective quietly left the premises. Glancing down at the lounging veteran he remarked, 'I've just brought tears to his eyes!'

A response was neither expected nor forthcoming so, without a backward glance, Joe headed for the Cozzens House Hotel. He knew that Bill would follow on and he had information to impart.

'That little pile of puke eventually proved to be very talkative. Turns out Marshal Pritchett is not just the peace officer of this piss pit,' he confided softly as they sat in the lobby. 'He also censors all the mail. Uses a mixture of threats and bribery without the telegraph company knowing a thing. He gets to see everything that comes into the office before the recipients do, so he's always one step ahead. Which means he knew what was going to happen to us yesterday, even if he wasn't party to it.'

His new employee regarded him warily. 'Seeing the smile on your face when you left that office, I reckoned you'd kicked some ass. Which also means that afore long the marshal's going to know that you know what he's about. If you get my drift,' he added dryly.

'That I do. The problem is, I don't have any idea what to do about it,' replied Joe with remarkable candour. It was rare indeed for him to admit to any shortcomings. There was something about Bill's assured manner that encouraged him to share confidences.

'Something'll come to you. Meantime, let's look in on your young friend,' that man responded. 'Who knows, he might fancy a nip of joy juice. That's if he's not already a laudanum addict.'

Joe knew that the older man was humouring him, but he took it in good part and together the two of them headed for the stairs. He was, after all, genuinely keen to see how his comrade was recovering. On reaching the corridor, they couldn't help but notice the large dried bloodstain on the boarding. It would take more than a bit of scrubbing to remove that. As they approached the door that Bill had forced, they heard the sound of hammering. A carpenter was replacing the shattered window. The man briefly glanced at them as they strode past. As yet they had not been approached to pay for the repairs, but it could not be long before someone plucked up the courage.

Dan's bedroom was at the rear of the hotel where it was

quieter. With his door being at the end of the corridor there was also less foot traffic. Happily summoning a broad smile, Joe entered the room. Everything was as they had left it. Dan appeared to be sound asleep, doubtless under the influence of the medicinal solution. The clean sheets were tucked high, so that only his unruly mop of fair hair was visible. It was the total lack of movement that brought a sudden chill to Joe's flesh.

Heart filled with dread, he rushed forward. Carefully pulling back the sheets, he recoiled in horror at the sight that met his eyes. A garbled cry escaped his lips as he took in the viciously severed flesh and the sheer quantity of sticky blood that coated Dan's chest. His throat had been cut with such force that his head was only kept in place by the support of the pillow. His eyes were wide open, staring glassily at the ceiling as though seeking a motive for his appalling fate. His mamma might not have raised him to get shot, but that fact hadn't saved him from the assassin's blade.

CHAPTER SIX

A terrible mixture of anger and grief swept over Joe as he stared around the room. He was crazy-eyed and almost beyond reason. While he had been out of the hotel, brutally intimidating an inconsequential clerk, his only real friend in the world had been slaughtered in his sickbed. Lurching blindly passed a shocked Bill Hickok, Joe reached the corridor. Someone was going to pay. At that moment in time he would have killed any man that came under his guns. Yet somehow, a fragment of logical thought penetrated his seething brain. Somebody must have seen the killer. He had to have had blood on his hands. The workman!

Joe's rapid footsteps alerted the carpenter, who gazed at him with apparent curiosity as he stormed into the room.

'What did you see?' he bellowed.

Interest turned to alarm as the man feigned ignorance. 'I didn't see nothing, mister!'

Bill had arrived in the room. He rapidly summed up the situation. Joe's mind, addled by grief, was incapable of careful reasoning, but not so his. 'If you won't tell us what you didn't see, tell us what you did.'

The man gazed at him in disbelief. Alarm began to give

way to belligerence. He was a large, powerful fellow with a hammer in his hand. 'Tricks with words don't cut it with me, mister. Back off and take your partner with you.'

Such obstruction proved too much for Joe. Cocking his Sharps, he thrust the muzzle towards the workman. It was lucky for that individual that the weapon did not have an iron socket bayonet attached.

'One man has already gone through that window, as well you know. If you don't talk, I'll make it two!'

A hammer was no answer to a breechloader, as the suddenly very scared workman realized. He was definitely going through the full gamut of emotions that morning. Inevitably it was he that had to back off and Joe followed on, all the time prodding the man's torso with his rifle barrel. Abruptly there was nowhere else to go. New panes of distorted glass were the only barrier between him and the street. A potentially fatal fall beckoned and the words began to flow. 'I'll talk, goddamn it. Just don't pop a cap on me. It was that big Irish bastard Sullivan that did it. He had blood on his hands when he left, just like you.'

It was true. Joe's hands had Dan's congealing blood on them, but his guilt was of a different kind. Shaking his head, as if trying to clear it, he took a step backward. He now had someone new to vent his anger on.

'What is Sullivan?' demanded Bill. 'Who does he answer to?'

The workman had sensed that the danger to him personally was passing. All he wanted then was to be rid of them.

'He works for Pritchett. He's a deputy.'

'I thought lawmen were sworn in to save lives, not take them,' remarked Bill dryly and then instantly regretted it. Joe fixed his wild-eyed stare on him before turning away and charging out of the room.

'Shit, that did it,' intoned Bill as he raced after his employer.

'Anybody asks, I never said a word,' yelled the workman after his persecutors.

Joe Wakefield bounded down the stairs and into the lobby. He was barely conscious of the startled looks that greeted his arrival. Although he could hear running footsteps behind him, he did not associate them with any particular threat. Forgetting all the rules that governed his profession, he ignored everyone and blundered out into the street. The only thing that filled his mind was the idea of drawing a fine bead on Deputy Sullivan. That man was going to die for what he had done to Dan. Whether it came hard or easy was up to him. As the sound of heavy breathing came from behind him, Joe said his piece without bothering to turn. 'You're either with me or against me in this, Hickok!'

Sure enough it was that man who replied. 'I was afraid you'd say that.'

The sudden devastating blow on the back of his head felt as though the sky was falling in. Overwhelming pain flooded over him and then everything simply went black.

Joe struggled desperately against some form of restraint. Something was pressing hard against his chest. Crying out, he snapped his eyes open. The strong daylight lanced in and hurt his nerves, but at least he could see. The imposing moustachioed figure of Bill Hickok loomed large as he leaned over him. He was holding the barrel of a much-abused Colt Navy, ready to use it as a club again if necessary. Bizarrely, it suddenly occurred to Joe that although his assailant was not particularly good-looking, he definitely possessed a roguish charm. He also had all his weight bearing down on his prisoner.

'Get off of me, goddamn it. That was one hell of a sock-dolager you gave me.'

Bill gazed down at him appraisingly. 'I ain't letting you up until you tell me you're over that conniption fit. If you'd bust into the marshal's office like that, you'd likely have got yourself kilt. Even if you'd got lucky, you wouldn't have been much better off. Killing a lawman is a sure way to trouble, even in these parts.'

Slowly the tension left Joe's body. The logic of that little speech was all too clear. And yes, the kill crazy fury had died down. What remained was a great sadness and an implacable desire for revenge. Regarding his captor calmly, he remarked, 'I've got my kilter back. You have my oath on it.'

Bill favoured him with a gentle smile and stood up. Holstering his revolver, he reached out and hauled Joe to his feet. That man groaned and swayed, but with the support of his companion remained upright. Gradually the nausea departed, until at last he was able to take in his surroundings. They were in a narrow side alley next to the hotel. As his awareness returned, so did his wits. Even as he spoke, he noticed that the other man was now in possession of Dan's new repeating rifle.

'We need to talk, but not here and not in the hotel. Let's head for the rail depot. There's bound to be an empty carriage we can use.'

'Now you're making sense,' responded Bill gratefully.

Ten minutes later they were ensconced in a deserted passenger car. Joe's written authorization from Thomas

Cartwright allowed him access to pretty much all parts of the Union Pacific operation.

'That shit-faced workman is the only person who knows that we've discovered Dan and he isn't going to talk,' reasoned Joe. 'Which means that we've got some time to think this through.' He deliberated for a moment and then continued. 'If the law in Omaha has been bought, then we need to find out who's put up the specie. I reckon the same son of a bitch is behind the train wrecking.'

'Can't argue with any of that,' replied his companion. 'Question is, how do we go about it?'

'We need to put a whole heap of pressure on that no-account marshal,' Joe stated forcefully. 'If he stands to lose his life or liberty, then he might could get to talking. Problem is, what we know and what we can prove are two whole different things.'

With that, a lengthy silence descended on the two men. They were faced with a thorny problem. Dan's murder was a hanging offence, but only if the killer could be brought to trial with a witness. Even then it wouldn't personally affect the marshal and it certainly wouldn't bring them any closer to identifying whoever was behind the derailments. Joe began to feel frustration building within him. He felt terribly responsible for the young man's death and harboured an extreme dread of having to confront Dan's poor mother in Hartford, Massachusetts with the news.

The brooding peace was shattered by a blasphemous oath, as Bill slapped his thigh. 'If you aren't already glad you've hired me, you will be now.'

Joe regarded him quizzically but remained silent.

'Mail tampering,' announced Bill with a theatrical flourish. 'That's how we get the son of a bitch. It's a federal offence to interfere with the post. The telegraph is a new-fangled form of mail. If there was a witness prepared to swear that Pritchett had been obtaining messages first by the use of bribes or threats, then we could have him arrested by a Deputy United States Marshal.'

Joe just stared at him as he absorbed what, initially, appeared to be a very fanciful idea. Yet the more he thought about it, the more he had to admit that he liked it.

'*Well*, what do you think?' demanded an impatient Bill Hickok, aggrieved that he hadn't received his deserved acclaim. 'You really are all shit and no sugar today!'

'I think it could just work, Bill,' the other man responded cautiously. 'The threat of federal prison should loosen Pritchett's tongue. But it will mean kidnapping and protecting a very reluctant witness. If the marshal realizes what we're about and gets his hands on him first, we wouldn't have a case.'

'Keeping him safe ain't going to be easy in this cesspool,' observed Bill. 'The marshal will have his ear to the ground. Your friend is proof of that.'

As the horrific scene in the hotel room flashed through his mind, Joe's features registered grim determination. He gestured around at their passenger carriage. 'He'd be safe enough in one of these ... if it was moving!'

The sun had just passed its zenith as James Butler Hickok sauntered over to the office of the Pacific Telegraph Company. The disabled veterans were still passing the time of day on the boardwalk. As he drew closer, one of them muttered confidentially, 'Young blowhard inside's not having a good day.'

Bill tilted back his wide-brimmed hat and replied in all seriousness, 'It's about to get worse.'

With that enigmatic comment, he entered the office. Conveniently there were no other customers. A somewhat battered young man was reading a message and clacking away on the telegraph key. He glanced up sourly at the newcomer. There was a crack in the spectacles that covered blackened eyes and his nose was red and angry. The liberal amount of cream spread over it testified to him having received some rudimentary medical attention.

'You'll have to wait,' he remarked testily with a notably nasal twang. 'I'm a busy man.'

'I guess there's just no rest for the wicked,' responded his suddenly very unwelcome visitor. A revolver had abruptly appeared in his right hand and was pointed unwaveringly at the clerk's head. 'May I know your name, young sir?'

That luckless individual's hand froze over the key. His saucer-like eyes were fixed on the gun muzzle as he stammered out a response. The injured nose had an unintentionally comic effect on his speech. 'My dame's Toby. P-p-please don't shoot me, mister.'

'Well hello, Toby,' Bill stated brightly. 'You and me are going to take a friendly stroll over to the railroad depot by way of the hotel. But first I want you to shut the office up and draw the blinds. Just as though you were going to take a little holiday.'

Watching as the telegraph office closed for business, Joe knew that it was time. Drawing in a deep, calming breath, he pivoted slightly so that he could scrutinize the marshal's office. Because the two were not in direct line of sight, there was no way that Pritchett could know that his 'messenger boy' had left unusually early. Having loitered for some time, Joe knew that there were only two lawmen on the premises. It was always possible that the marshal had one of his men outside on watch, but Joe hadn't spotted anyone and in any case it was unlikely.

Pritchett couldn't know that there was a specific threat against him.

Although the office had iron bars on all the windows, the blinds were up to allow in plenty of natural light. The marshal was sipping a cup of coffee. The two men were obviously about to indulge in a late lunch, as his power-fully built deputy had only just arrived with what had looked like a food hamper. If his name was Sullivan, he was about to get more than a piece of pie in his gut. He bore no resemblance to the brute that had backed Pritchett in the eating house, which meant that there was at least one more deputy on the loose. Joe knew that he was taking a great risk, confronting the lawmen in their own lair, but he was counting on the advantage of surprise to see him through.

Stepping lightly off the boardwalk, he strolled casually across the street. His Sharps, with its thirty-inch barrel, was held loosely at his side. Its hammer was on half cock to prevent any accidental discharge. Joe had decided against exchanging it for his murdered friend's Winchester. He was comfortably familiar with his big 'cap 'n ball' rifle and he well knew that it looked far more intimidating at close range. Besides, Bill appeared to be quite taken with the new-fangled weapon.

Reaching the door, he stopped and politely knocked softly on the glass before entering. As expected, the two men looked over at him without any sign of alarm. They both wore gunbelts but their hands were otherwise occu-pied. The marshal had obviously temporarily removed his earlier that morning before entering the eating house, in an effort to lull his two intended victims into a sense of false security. Joe deliberately avoided eye contact, fearful that they would notice the fire in his gaze. Instead he chose to glance casually around the office, before moving in closer. Pritchett had a mouthful of cold meat, but still couldn't resist a scornful greeting. 'Hey, it's the railroad detective, whatever one of those is. Next thing you know they'll be sending in the Pinkertons, ha ha.'

'Why on earth should they want to do that, marshal?' Joe asked lightly, before abruptly eyeballing the deputy. 'Might your name be Sullivan?'

Confusion registered on that man's bovine features. 'What if it. . . ?'

Joe slammed the rifle muzzle into Sullivan's belly with tremendous force. With an agonized cry, the deputy doubled over and staggered back into his boss, thereby preventing that man from drawing his revolver. Timing his next move to perfection, Joe used a two-handed grip to smash the stock up into his victim's unprotected face. Allowing the momentum to carry him on, he then executed a complete pirouette and so came to rest before the two lawmen. With an ominous click, he retracted the hammer to full cock.

Deputy Sullivan had tumbled back towards the empty cells, where he hit the floor with a resounding thump. His head came to rest in a mess of blood and shattered teeth. Thereafter, his body was completely still. Whether dead or alive, he was definitely out of the confrontation. Under the circumstances, Marshal Pritchett remained remarkably cool. Calmly regarding the gaping muzzle, he remarked, 'You've only got the one shot, mister!'

'It's all I need,' was Joe's confident response.

Accepting the truth in that, Pritchett tried again. 'If you've kilt him, you'll hang, Wakefield.'

He knows my name, Joe realized before responding. 'Not if you're in the custody of a US Marshal, Pritchett. Mail tampering's a federal offence and I've got a witness who'll point the finger at you.'

The town marshal regarded him in total silence. His square-jawed face remained impassive. The drooping moustache didn't even twitch. Only a slight narrowing of his eyes suggested that he was actually under pressure. Finally he allowed himself a cold smile. 'Well, well, you have been busy. So what do you want?'

'I want the name of the man behind the attacks on the Union Pacific. I caught up with some of your thugs. Before Jake died he talked.'

Pritchett gave a derisive snort. 'That's not the way I heard it. Anyhoo, it makes no odds. You're getting nothing out of me. It's maybe two weeks before a federal officer is due here. Even if you have got a witness, you couldn't protect him that long. This is still my town, Wakefield.'

'Not if I kill you it isn't.'

'In cold blood? You haven't got the grit, boy. Besides, if I did happen to turn up dead, you'd never get that name, now would you?'

He had a point and Joe knew it. The corrupt marshal had effectively called his bluff. Unless it wasn't actually a bluff. If he and Hickok could get their witness to safety, everything would change. At the very least a deal could be done!

Mind made up, Joe favoured Pritchett with a knowing smile. 'Unbuckle that gun-belt and let it slide to the ground.'

'And if I don't?'

'Then I'll wing you. This cannon will likely take your

arm off at close range. Then you can join those poor bastards out in the street, just waiting around to die.'

The lawman's eyes were like flints as he weighed up his
options. Finally he shrugged and did as instructed. 'Now
what?' he barked.

'Now you open a cell and lock yourself in.'

Pritchett appeared on the point of protesting, but
thought better of it. There was little point. Everything had
already been said. Grabbing a heavy key from his desk, he
entered the nearest cell, locked himself in and then dismissively tossed the iron instrument back on to its resting
place. Joe gestured with his Sharps for the lawman to back
off, before checking the lock. Satisfied, he picked up the
key and then retreated to the door. At no time did he take
his eyes away from Pritchett's menacing figure.

For what it was worth, the imprisoned marshal did
manage to get the last word. 'You're a dead man walking,
Wakefield!'

CHAPTER SEVEN

As Joe hurriedly made his way over to the railroad depot, he had a number of problems eating at him. He would have given anything to know the identity of Jake's assassin. Bill Hickok's possession of a duster coat had remained in his thoughts, even though that man's recent actions had surely proven his loyalty. Then again, for a man prepared to fight over a mere window seat, he had remained remarkably placid when grossly insulted by the marshal. It was all too much. His head was hurting. Bill really shouldn't have hit him so hard.

Joe found the two men lurking near the engine sheds. Bill was dismissively ignoring the curious glances of the many passing railroad workers. Flashily dressed and supremely self-confident, with his shiny new Winchester and a brace of revolvers, he projected an aura of latent violence that was hard to ignore. Conversely, Toby, in his blood-spattered, store-bought clothes, looked singularly out of place and ill at ease in such surroundings. His discomfiture increased tenfold when he spotted his erstwhile assailant striding towards him. A hand instinctively flew up to shield his damaged nose. Behind the spectacles, his eyes watered as though in anticipation of another vicious blow.

'Don't hit me again, mister. For pity's sake,' he wailed. 'I done told you everything you wanted.'

Ignoring the pitiful outburst, Bill inquired, 'So how did it go?'

'It could have panned out better,' Joe replied tersely. 'Pritchett's locked in his own jail. He just flat-out wouldn't co-operate. The deputy's out cold or dead.' Pointing at the snivelling clerk, he continued, 'The only way this can work is if we leave town, fast, if you get my meaning.'

Oh, Bill understood all right. He had Dan's Winchester chambered up and ready. 'Way I see it, there's any number of routes out of this shithole.'

He wasn't wrong. Even without purchasing mounts from the livery, they could head north or south on a Missouri River steamboat, or travel east on the Chicago, Rock Island and Pacific Railroad.

'We can forget the river,' Joe responded firmly. 'It doesn't take us anywhere we want to be. And those sons of bitches on the Rock Island won't take my bona fides, so we'd have to pay.'

'Which leaves a supply train back to the railhead.'

'Yeah, it does,' deliberated Joe. 'We get our witness here back to Colonel Cartwright and he can summon a US Marshal. With the Union Pacific involved, the federal authorities will have to take notice. Pritchett'll have no choice then. He'll have to talk to avoid jail and I can go back to hunting buffalo.'

'Witness?' piped up Toby. 'Witness to what?' Mystified, he gazed from one to the other until he recalled the reference to Omaha's marshal and suddenly took Joe's meaning. His damaged features turned ashen and normal speech was a noticeable problem. 'I'm *d*ot speaking out against Pritchett. He'll butcher me like a steer.' He had been involved with the people who had carried out the atrocity in the hotel room. He had obviously been deeply shocked by what he had seen, and rightly so.

The .44/.40-rifle bullet slammed into the timber doorframe of the engine shed. Bill grabbed the terrified clerk and pulled him inside. 'You ought to be careful what you wish for,' he remarked drolly.

More shots rang out, but for the time being the three men were protected by the walls of the huge building. The maintenance workers nearby had swiftly downed tools and retreated to the rear of the shed. Joe forced himself to look objectively at their surroundings. The engine sheds provided all-weather cover for maintenance work on the locomotives. Tracks ran from the buildings and merged with the single line heading west. On that line was an apparently fully laden supply train. The passenger car that they had recently occupied was at the rear of it. That train was quite obviously their only way out.

Pushing Toby down on to the ground out of harm's way, Joe sized up his chances. If he could reach the nearside of the train, he would be out of sight to the gunmen.

'You're going to have to cover me, Bill. I've got the papers that can get that engine moving, with us as passengers.'

'Uh huh,' was the only audible response, but his companion obviously fully understood Joe's intentions, because he tucked the rifle butt tightly into his shoulder and cocked the hammer. Drawing in a deep breath, Bill stepped up to the doorframe and swung the twenty-four-inch barrel outside. He fired off a shot and then kept on firing, working the under-lever like a man possessed.

As the first detonation rang out, Joe ran for the safety

of the train. A variety of balls and bullets kicked up the earth around him, but the shooting was wild and none struck flesh. Bill's covering fire was very effective, but it was then that something was said that had frightening implications.

Marshal Deke Pritchett felt a truly murderous rage boiling up inside of him. No lawman relishes being incarcerated in his own jailhouse, but that was only a part of it. He was in very real danger of losing both his lucrative position and his freedom. If that poxed little cur Toby could be coerced into testifying before a judge, then everything would unravel. The Union Pacific had enough political clout to get a conviction. The choice then would be to serve hard time in a federal penitentiary or make a deal that would undoubtedly place the marshal in mortal danger.

As the cell door swung open, courtesy of a spare key, he dismissively stepped over Sullivan's prone figure and bellowed at his two remaining deputies. 'Nobody locks Deke Pritchett in his own jail! Just nobody! Round up everybody with a gun. I reckon we've got a train to catch.'

Within minutes, an armed posse was milling around the clapboard buildings bordering the depot.

'I want them dead or alive,' demanded the marshal. 'You hear me? I want them dead!'

The temporary deputies owned a variety of muzzle-loaders, breech-loaders and repeating weapons. So long as the town was paying for all ammunition expended, they were happy to blaze away. The first poorly aimed shot resulted in the three fugitives retreating to an engine shed, but Pritchett knew that they wouldn't stay there. 'Watch out, boys. Anybody makes a move, you let 'em have it.'

Those words were barely out of his mouth before a rifle barrel appeared and began to spit lead at an alarming rate. Bullets smacked into the buildings where he and his men were congregating. At the same time, a tall, well-made character burst out of the shed and sprinted for the supply train.

'Bring down that bastard,' commanded Pritchett, but the accurate covering fire had disrupted his men's aim. Their projectiles only succeeded in striking the ground around the fleeing figure. It was then that the marshal directed a singularly strange question at Joe Wakefield's companion. 'Just whose side are you on, Hickok?'

Joe heard the shouted accusation but he was too busy running for his life to give it any immediate consideration. Like an untreated wound, it would fester until at last it demanded attention. Even when he reached the safety of the passenger car he had to keep moving. It was a long supply train, heavily loaded with much-needed rails and crossties. The locomotive looked to be fired up, but the amount of steam being emitted appeared pretty lacklustre.

A grimy, fleshy face appeared from inside of the wooden cab. 'Thank God,' intoned Joe. At least the engineer was present. Increasing speed, the railroad detective dashed up to the side of the imposing Iron Horse.

'We need to get moving, now!' he hollered up at the surprised Union Pacific employee.

'You don't say. And just who the hell are you?' came the belligerent response.

There was no time for debate. Grabbing hold of the handrails. Joe hauled himself up into the cab. The engineer was a stocky, middle-aged fellow, who obviously resented the intrusion. Pulling a buffalo-hide folder from his jacket pocket, Joe opened out the contents. 'Can you read?' he demanded.

'I've been lettered since I was ten,' came the indignant reply.

'Good for you. Read this!'

The engineer perused the impressive letter of authorization from Colonel Cartwright. Even as he did so, the sound of gunfire came from the buildings behind them.

'Just what the hell's happening back there?'

'My companions are under attack from men involved in the train wreckings. We have to get out of here, now! You need to back this train up to the shed, so the others can get on without taking any lead.'

The engineer's confrontational manner had dissipated, but he made no move to do as instructed. He looked from the letter to its owner and then shrugged regretfully. 'I'd surely like to help, young feller. I surely would. But this train can't go anywhere yet.'

Anger was never far below the surface and Joe could feel his hackles start to rise. 'What's stopping you?' he demanded impatiently.

'I've no fireman,' came the simple response. 'He's in the privy with gut-ache. Been there half the morning and I sure ain't going in after him!'

Joe gawped at him in disbelief. The whole supply train was immobilized because one man was taking a lengthy shit. 'Well you've got a new fireman now,' he proclaimed forcefully. 'Me!'

So saying, he propped his Sharps in the corner, pulled on a pair of discarded gloves and unlatched the firebox. Before the engineer could protest, he began heaving lumps of wood from the tender on to the grates inside it.

61

Despite the noise in the cab, he could hear the sound of rapid firing.

'Get this damn machine moving, mister,' ordered Joe.

The engineer's head jerked, as he seemed to suddenly come to terms with the reality of the situation. Without further delay, he moved over to his post. Checking the steam pressure gauge, he called over. 'Keep shoving it in. I kept the fire going myself, so it won't take long.'

Then he checked another gauge and abruptly froze, as though struck by a horrendous thought. 'We can't go anywhere! We haven't taken on near enough water yet. Without it, the firebox could melt and we'd get a blowback of high-pressure steam into the cab. It'd likely kill us both!'

CHAPTER EIGHT

James Butler Hickok leapt back behind the doorframe. The tubular magazine was empty, but his Winchester had served its purpose. Joe had reached the temporary safety of the train and was running for the locomotive. Bill grunted in satisfaction and began to feed more cartridges through the Yellow Boy's loading gate. It really was an excellent weapon, but it did use ammunition at a frightening rate. Thankfully, he had taken the time to retrieve Dan's burlap bag containing boxes of rimfires from beside the murdered man's bed. He had again gazed down on Dan's young face and felt a surge of anger that such an affable young fellow should be slaughtered in his sickbed.

More shots crashed out and a variety of projectiles slammed into the building. Bill felt a strong urge to respond, but managed to resist it. Blazing away at their assailants would serve no purpose and only waste valuable ammunition. So long as Pritchett's posse stayed amongst the buildings, they were no immediate threat. Unfortunately the marshal fully realized that fact!

Deke Pritchett savagely chewed on a fresh plug of tobacco. Whether he gained any pleasure from it was doubtful. His mind was a seething cauldron as he weighed up the situation before him. They couldn't pursue Wakefield because that cursed gunhand in the engine shed would surely bring them down. Therefore they had to tackle Hickok first. He didn't know what the man's game was, but as far as he was concerned it was shoot to kill from there on in. The building was too solid to penetrate with lead. Since the lawman didn't possess any siege artillery, that only left fire. Burning down the Union Pacific's property was far from sensible, but he was too far gone to care. Having sent a man off for some kerosene lamps, he was soon ready to proceed. Producing some lucifers from his pocket, he threw them at the nearest deputy and snarled, 'Get those poxy lamps lit, Teague. The rest of you keep that whoreson's head down. He's too damned handy with that repeater!'

Concentrated musketry rattled out, as every man aimed at the engine shed. It never occurred to Pritchett that there might be other innocent men sheltering in the building and he wouldn't have altered his plans if it had. The tainted lawman glanced sharply over at the subordinate charged with burning the two fugitives out.

Deputy Teague appeared to be far from happy with his new role. His hands trembled at their task, but he well knew that nobody gainsaid Marshal Pritchett when that man's blood was up. Behind the curved glass all the wicks were burning handsomely and it was time. Pritchett nodded decisively and then gestured for his man to advance. The overwhelming fusillade had stifled any return fire from the huge shed. Teague rushed forward carrying two lamps in each hand.

Although initially driven on by fear, that man unexpectedly realized that he was actually going to make it.

Exhilaration lightened his step and suddenly he was there. Triumphantly, he slammed the lamps into the side of the building. As they shattered, the kerosene ignited on the rough-cut timber. Flames soared up the side of the shed and Teague jubilantly turned away to begin his dash back. The other deputies considered it a job well done and instinctively slackened their fire.

From the entrance of the building, a rifle barrel swiftly appeared. Its owner drew a bead on the fleeing man and fired. The bullet caught Teague smack between the shoulder blades and for a brief moment actually assisted him in his escape. Then he stumbled and coughed blood and suddenly it was all over. As the deputy fell to earth, his companions howled out their collective anger. Pritchett didn't bother to join in. The fate of one man was irrelevant. The fire had taken hold. That damned shootist could either take a bullet or burn to death. As for young Toby, well his tenure at the Pacific Telegraph Company was definitely coming to an end!

Bill Hickok felt a temporary glow of satisfaction as he withdrew from the entrance. The tarnal fire-starter had been despatched to hell. Yet unfortunately, that man had achieved his aim. The side wall was ablaze and soon it would be the whole building. The other occupants of the shed began to hurl abuse at him for bringing such peril upon them, but he paid them no mind. The sound of a locomotive in motion had suddenly seized his attention. And yes, it was true. The passenger car that Joe had bolted for was actually backing up towards them.

Grasping Toby by the arm, Bill hauled him to his feet. The bruised and bewildered clerk appeared to be numb to his circumstances, as though the whole situation was just too much to take in. Bill looked at him closely and shook his head. Without warning, he slapped the young man sharply across the face. The shock of the blow brought fresh tears to his eyes, but it also jolted him out of his stupor.

'Listen to me,' the gunfighter snarled. 'When I say move, you run full chisel for that engine. Don't stop for anything, you hear?'

Toby's nose had started to bleed again. He gazed up into the hard eyes of his tormentor. How had he got himself into all this? Timber was crackling under the assault of the flames and he could feel tremendous heat emanating from the wall. One thing was for sure, he couldn't stay there. He hurriedly nodded his acquiescence, absurdly conscious of the droplets of fresh blood that splashed on to his jacket.

The rear of the train was crawling closer. Bill cocked his reloaded Winchester. He knew that even on reaching the cover of the passenger car, their troubles would be far from over. If they boarded it, they would still be vulnerable to any sustained gunfire. Their only chance was to head up the track to the solidity of the locomotive. Unfortunately that would give Pritchett and his deputies the chance to advance on the train as well.

Bill was just about to give the word to move when an idea struck him. Turning, he looked over at the workmen unhappily assembled at the rear of the shed. He pointed his rifle muzzle at the biggest of them and called out. 'You there, if you want to escape with your life, come over here.'

A big bear of a man shambled over until he was standing directly in front of him. The fellow glared down at Bill belligerently, but that man appeared unconcerned as he addressed him. 'If we can get out of here, those law dogs will pursue us and you'll be free to vacate this hellhole. So it would behove you to help us. The flames are nearly through this wall.' Pointing at a heavy crosstie lying by the track, he continued. 'Throw that through the wall to draw their fire and we'll be off. Savvy?'

The workman appeared to be slow-witted but he savvy'd all right. Grasping the heavy wooden bar in his great paws, he hurled it with all his considerable strength at the weakened timber. As it smashed through the wall, sparks showered everywhere. Luckily the workman had the wit to back off fast, because Pritchett's men instinctively thought it was a breakout and unleashed a hail of lead.

Grabbing Toby, Bill charged across the short open space to the temporary safety of the passenger car. Ahead of them, Joe's torso appeared from the cab as he waved them on. The train had come to a halt before beginning a slow forward motion.

'Run like the devil's coming for you,' Bill yelled at his unhappy companion. He knew that it wouldn't be long before the deputies had them in their sights. As the engine gathered speed, it became a race for life that they just had to win. Together they pounded along by the side of the track. To their left were the flat cars loaded high with thirty-foot-long rails. They would stop any number of bullets, but unfortunately their pursuers would soon be directly behind them. Both men were sweating freely under the strong June sunshine as they finally came level with the cab. Unbelievably they had still not attracted any gunfire and there was even a friendly face beaming down at them.

'You took your sweet time,' Joe remarked as he helped them both aboard.

*

'You're shooting at shadows, you morons,' bawled Marshal Pritchett as he witnessed the two fugitives slip across the gap to safety. The sudden explosion of sparks from the blazing wall had caught them all off guard. What was more, the train was moving again. Only this time it was heading out of town. If that telegraph clerk evaded him, then his whole world would tumble down like a pack of cards. And, since Pritchett couldn't stop the train there and then, he would have to board it with as many of his men as possible. Mind made up, he leapt forward and hollered at his men to follow. The locomotive was remorselessly picking up speed now. Time was short.

Panting from the unaccustomed exertion, the lawman desperately closed on the rear of the train. He was a big man who usually let other people do the running and all this activity didn't suit him one bit.

'Get up into that passenger car,' he commanded. Even as he uttered the words, he was aware that several of his men were drifting. Some of the temporary deputies wanted no part of an open-ended gun battle on the move. They had only signed on to take pot shots at an outnumbered prey, yet already one man was dead. God alone knew where it would all end.

Chet Parsons was the only remaining regular deputy. He was the vicious bruiser of a man who had silently backed his boss's play in the eating house. It was he who reached the handrail first and pulled himself aboard. Three more men, all of them close to Pritchett and too scared of him to bolt, also made it. By then the marshal was winded and the bastard train was pulling away from him. With one final tremendous effort, he lunged for the handrail at the rear of the carriage. As his clawed right hand gripped tight, he stumbled and his feet dragged on the crossties within the track. Cursing, he dropped his rifle and desperately reached out with his left hand.

Of the four men clustered on the rear open-air platform, only Parsons felt any loyalty to Deke Pritchett. Although motivated solely by greed, it was enough to create a bond of sorts. So it fell to him to grab the outstretched hand and heave his boss up on to the rail. Aided by sheer brute force, that man fell forward on to the deck like a sack and lay in an inert heap, completely unable to speak. Disappointed that he had actually made it, the other three grudgingly gave him some space. They were convinced that his baleful presence was sure to guarantee more violence.

Parsons and two of the reluctant posse moved forward into the passenger car, leaving one man outside. That individual innocently allowed curiosity to get the better of him. Moving to the extreme left, he descended two steps, took hold of a handrail and leaned out. The ground was moving beneath him at quite a rate. He felt exhilaration at the sheer speed. It really was the only way to travel. With the railroad depot fast receding and the welcome breeze ruffling his hair, he took a look over to the front of the train. A movement at the side of the cab caught his eye, but by then it was too late.

The .52-calibre ball struck his lower jaw and completely shattered it, before exploding out of the back of his skull. Choking on teeth and bone fragments, the deputy swung back towards the deck just as his grip gave way. His now lifeless body tumbled away from the train and down to the earth. Spots of blood and brain matter had spattered over Pritchett's recumbent form. That man wiped his own sweat and the deputy's detritus from his face and cursed very softly, mainly because that was all he could manage. Someone was going to goddamn pay for all of this!

Josiah Wakefield blew into the breach of his Sharps rifle before allowing himself a smile of satisfaction. That really had been a peach of a shot. Firing from a platform in motion at another moving object required a deal of skill and experience. Unfortunately, he was almost certain that there would be other men aboard the train and that the corrupt marshal was sure to be amongst them.

Glancing around the now crowded cab, he pondered his next move. It was then that Pritchett's ambiguous question came back to haunt him. Just how well could be trust the self-assured pistol fighter standing before him? Well there was no time like the present, but first he had to delegate some responsibility. Fixing his gaze on Toby, he remarked, 'From now on you're the fireman and you answer to the engineer. Get stoking!'

That luckless individual peered at him through his cracked, bottle-bottomed glasses and whined, 'But I don't know anything about trains.'

'Well now's the time to learn,' remarked Joe, thrusting the fireman's thick gloves at him. Toby accepted them with poor grace. The brutal handling that he had earlier received still rankled, but that very memory ensured that he at least made an effort.

Joe had discovered that Toby's new boss was called Barnaby Jones. After his initial reluctance to co-operate, that man had accepted the situation and had got the engine moving. The shortage of water had required a calculated gamble on his part and the problem would remain with them.

Now that Joe had his hands free, there was still that one

70

very important consideration to address. Moving out of Toby's way, he gestured for Bill to join him and then cut straight to the chase.

To the accompaniment of the familiar chuffing sound, as the exhaust steam escaped through the blastpipe and up through the chimney, he said, 'We left Omaha without taking on water. Barnaby says there's an overhead tank at Fremont, so we have to stop there. Otherwise none of us will walk away from this train.' Joe scrutinized Bill carefully as he continued. 'Yet we can't do that under the guns of whoever's in the passenger car.'

The other man needed no prompting. 'So we have to clean out that nest of vipers first.'

'Yep. But first I need to know one thing.' So saying, Joe stepped in closer, so that he was almost nose-to-nose with the other man. His hand rested on the smooth butt of his Colt Army. He had taken Bill's advice and removed the holster flap. As their eyes locked, he asked the question, 'Just whose side are you on, Hickok?'

That man's eyes narrowed slightly as he took in the determination on Joe's face. For a long moment they regarded each other in relative silence. It could only ever be *relative*, because there was a constant background din from the firebox, boiler and running gear of the massive locomotive. Finally Bill Hickok supplied a reply, but it was not one likely to ease Joe's concern.

'Don't get all wrathy with me, Wakefield. You might be a hunky-dory shot with a long gun, but you'd be dead before you got that piece out of its holster. Study on it!'

It was not what Joe had hoped for, but he resolved to stand firm. Not that that was possible with the damnable swaying of the locomotive. The man opposite was apparently so confident that he had made no move towards his

Colt Navys, which in itself was unnerving. He tried again.

'You accepted my offer of work. I need to know that I can trust you. So I'm asking you, what did Pritchett mean?'

Bill sighed, as he was in the habit of doing when a problem arose. The bloody man in front of him just didn't know when to back down. Yet he also happened to be right. An explanation was required. His features remained as hard as granite, but when he spoke his tone had altered. 'I'd had a bad run at the faro table. Deke Pritchett offered me a job. Something to do with the Union Pacific. I agreed, but nothing came of it and I took no money from him.'

'You haven't had any from me, yet. So how do I know I can trust you?'

'Because I saved your life yesterday. And besides, I've decided I like you. I don't kill somebody that I like!' With that, his face creased into a broad smile and he jerked his head towards the rear of the train. 'Come on. What say we see just who's back there?'

Joe was feeling a lot happier, but he wasn't quite finished. 'Fair enough, but I need Pritchett alive. If he dies, all this is for nothing. Do you understand me?'

'Oh, I understand you all right,' Bill responded agreeably. 'But if it comes down to his life or mine, I'll parole him straight to Jesus!'

CHAPTER NINE

The two men climbed, one on either side, on to the swaying tender and immediately regretted it. Unlike the iron rails on the flat cars behind, the lumps of rough-cut wood that it contained were not chained down. They also realized that once on top, they would be in plain sight and very vulnerable.

'We need you up there with that buffalo gun,' shouted Bill. He had discarded Dan's Winchester in favour of his own belt guns, allowing him more flexibility. 'Then I can move on to the flat cars while you cover me.'

Nodding his agreement, Joe scrabbled awkwardly over the firewood. Splinters tore at his hands and he repeatedly banged his knees, but finally he reached the rear of the tender. Dropping flat proved to be even more uncomfortable, but at least his Sharps Rifle could now cover the full length of the train. He counted eight flat cars stacked high with rails, which meant that the barely visible passenger car behind them was roughly eighty-five yards away. At such range anyone showing his face back there would get a lethal shock.

Deke Pritchett knew nothing of the engine's water shortage; otherwise he would have sat tight. As it was, he presumed that the train would speed full throttle for the railhead and so had to be stopped at all costs.

'Get out there and pop some caps,' he commanded. 'Just don't hit the engineer or we're all mustered out.'

None of the three men assembled before him in the passenger car showed any inclination to step outside.

'At least one of those cockchafers knows how to shoot,' complained the permanent deputy, Parsons. His brutalized features suggested that he had years of casual violence behind him and even Pritchett struggled to browbeat him without damned good reason. 'If we show our heads above those rails it'll be like a turkey shoot.'

The marshal glared at him, but could not deny the truth in his words. Yet they couldn't just languish in the stifling carriage. Looking for an easier target, he rounded on one of the two remaining posse members. The man had the look of a city gent, whose prosperous times were long behind him. Had the pockets of his soiled waistcoat been bulging with greenbacks, there would have been no need for him to sign on for a manhunt. He sported a faded bowler hat, worn at what he thought was a raffish angle. Such headgear was not uncommon in the West and had probably been brought out from some tidewater city by its owner.

'Take that purdy bonnet off. Get outside and raise it up above the rails,' Pritchett instructed. 'Slowly, mind, as though you're swimming in molasses.' Turning to the others, he continued, 'Get out on either side of the flat car and make ready to move forward. There'll be plenty to hold on to.'

'What are you gonna be doing?' inquired Parsons, clearly unhappy with the plan.

'I'll be waiting on events,' came back the unhelpful reply. 'Now get your sorry hides moving!'

*

74

Joe tried to relax and ignore the logs that dug painfully into various parts of his body. Being higher up, he was at the mercy of the choking smoke blowing back from the stack. His rifle, hammer on full cock, was trained on a point just above the centre of the rails on the rearmost flat car. He had already squeezed the first trigger, so that the slightest hint of pressure on the second would send the ball on its way. The last that he had seen of Bill was when that man climbed over the rear of the tender and dropped down on to the couplings. These connected all the cars to the locomotive, controlled the slack between the cars and took the tensional load of pulling them all. Bill's intention was to work his way down the side of the cars, using the iron rails for handholds.

An annoying bead of sweat trickled down Joe's forehead, but that was instantly banished from his thoughts when he saw a semi-circular object rise up behind the rails. A bowler hat! The question was, did there happen to be a head under it or was it purely a ruse? Seconds past and it rose slightly higher. There was no help for it, he would have to fire.

Joe lined up dead centre on the faded object and squeezed the second trigger. A fleck of copper flew back at him as the rifle discharged. The powder smoke was wiped away by the wind and so he saw the hat fly into the air and then disappear. The complete absence of blood and brains indicated that he had been duped, but it also told him what Pritchett's thugs were about. Even as he pushed another linen cartridge into the breech, he was shouting out a warning. 'They're coming along the sides, Bill!'

The shabby bowler hat flew up and then off the train, lost to its owner for ever but it had served its purpose. Pritchett bellowed out to the two men clinging to the rails. 'One of those scum-bellies is on the tender. Get forward. We'll follow on behind and cover you.'

Drawing his revolver, he gestured for the now hatless deputy to follow his companion. By so doing, the marshal ensured that he followed the far more capable Chet Parsons. With two of them advancing in tandem on either side of the train, they were bound to flank somebody. It never occurred to him that both of his opponents might favour the high ground.

James Butler Hickok was squatting over the creaking couplings in a most undignified manner when he heard the loud detonation above him. Joe's shouted warning followed that and he knew then what he had to do. Using both hands, he clambered up on to the pile of iron rails. The swaying of the car was disconcerting. It meant that he would always need at least one hand to assist in staying aloft. Joe was immediately behind him, so he moved carefully off to his right to allow a clear field of fire.

Stretching before Bill were the heavily loaded flat cars, followed by the apparently empty passenger carriage. That could only mean that Pritchett and his gun thugs were moving up the sides. Dropping down on to the unyielding rails, he crawled over to the edge and took a rapid glance down the length of the train. Sure enough, the deputy from the eating house was already moving on to the second car in, followed by the marshal himself. A rapid check on the other side revealed a similar picture. Thanks to Joe's Sharps, those men were denied the high ground and there was a chance to cause some mischief.

Bill clambered back to the edge opposite the tender and called over to his companion. 'Reckon you could shoot the chains out on the third wagon in from the passenger car? It'll possibly mean losing a load of rails, but it might could even the odds out.'

Joe smiled as he contemplated the task. 'At that range I could even part your flowing hair without hitting you!'

The other man nodded sagely at such obvious braggadocio. 'Better get to it, then,' he suggested mildly before turning away. Moving off to his right, he kept low and headed off down the train at speed. He fully intended to be on hand when those links were severed.

Joe drew a fine bead on the thick iron chain at the top of the stack of rails. At such range, the only complication was the constant movement of the train, but by careful observation he was able to compensate for that. Seeing that his companion was almost in place, he drew in a shallow breath and then fired. The target was momentarily obscured by powder smoke, but that mattered not. He knew without any doubt that he had hit the link. And sure enough the chain had parted.

Bill Hickok possessed natural athletic ability, which he was showing off to the full. By leaping from the top of one pile of rails to the next, he had just landed on the fifth car down when the Sharps discharged. As the heavy ball struck home, cries of alarm went up from both sides of the next load of rails. Now was his chance. Drawing his right-hand Colt, Bill kept low and moved rapidly forward.

All his efforts were rewarded when he suddenly found himself gazing down on Chet Parson's brutish form. That man had just reached the couplings between his car and Bill's. Catching sight of the shape above him, Chet desperately attempted to aim his huge Colt Dragoon revolver. He didn't even get close. Bill's Navy Six crashed out to deadly effect. The .36-calibre ball struck the deputy squarely in the chest. At such range it was sufficient to lift a man off his feet. In Chet's case the result was far worse. His clawed left hand retained a tenuous grip on an iron rail, but his trigger finger contracted with the shock of the blow. The massive 'horse pistol' detonated point blank into an iron rail. The soft lead ball struck unyielding metal, flattened out and then ricocheted straight back into his ample belly. The projectile had effectively become a piece of shrapnel and tore through his innards, doing terrible damage. With a wail of uncomprehending agony, Chet fell backwards from the train. His broken body hit the earth and rolled several times before finally coming to rest.

Chet Parson's abrupt demise coincided with another completely unforeseen event. As the engineer had predicted, the boiler was getting low on water. As a result of this the crown of the firebox had become dangerously exposed. The only answer was to slow down, reduce pressure and limp carefully into Fremont. So it was that Barnaby Jones chose that particular moment to apply the brakes. The conscientious engineer could never have foreseen the chaos that his innocent decision would create. As sparks flew from the driving wheels, the whole train jerked in response. The cargo of thirty-foot-long iron rails was kept securely in place by stout chains: except on one particular flat car.

Marshal Deke Pritchett was beginning to feel a long way from home. Struggling along the outside of a moving train was a new and unpleasant experience for him. The ground swept past at unnerving speed, so he kept his eyes firmly on Parson's back. That man was well in front and seemed to have no fear of their situation. Pritchett had just climbed on to the third car in, when there was a tremendous metallic crack and a thick length of chain flew in front of him.

'Sweet Jesus!' he yelled out in alarm. His heart jumped with shock, as he irrationally expected the huge rails to fall outwards, taking him with them. Of course inertia kept them in place and would continue to do so unless there were any sudden movements. Belatedly realizing this, he moved forward again to the sound of the loose chain jangling by the track.

Suddenly there was a loud gunshot, followed by an even deeper report. Up ahead, his deputy emitted an anguished cry and fell away from the side of the train. As his body rushed past, Pritchett saw that the whole torso was covered in blood. Rapidly glancing forward, he was just in time to see Bill Hickok on the next car. Impotent anger surged through him. He was on the point of hurling out an angry challenge when the whole train gave a tremendous jolt. Clinging on for dear life, the marshal felt the massive cargo shift position. There was the sound of rending metal and a terrified scream came from the far side of the car.

Joe was the only man behind the engine unaffected by the sudden decrease in speed. He saw Bill lose his balance and fall heavily on to the rails. Some animal instinct ensured that he didn't drop his revolver, but he lay unmoving as though badly winded. Leaving his heavy rifle in the tender, Joe clambered awkwardly to his feet. Easing himself over the side, he dropped down on to the couplings. He knew that there was probably at least one man on either side of the flat cars, so he decided to follow Bill over the top.

Utilizing the ladder-like configuration of the rails, Joe was soon on top of the first car. The train had settled down to a steady, much slower pace. He drew his Colt Army and carefully advanced in thirty-foot relays. All the time there were desperate cries for help coming from off to his left. It was only as he drew closer to Bill's position that he discovered their source. Thanks to his carefully judged shot, some of the rails had shifted on the sixth car. One of the reluctant deputies was clinging for dear life to a topmost rail that had swivelled out away from the train. As he drew closer to the edge, Joe could not resist sniggering at the man's predicament.

Agonizing pain suddenly lanced through his left hand. Never in his entire life had he ever experienced anything like it. The gunshot had seemingly come out of nowhere. Fighting the nausea that threatened to overwhelm him, Joe took a leap of faith and jumped across the void. He sensed rather than saw the man beneath him, as that individual crouched over the couplings. Landing on the sixth car, he twisted around and fired down into the gap. His ball went wide, but it had the effect of disrupting the deputy's second shot. That projectile flew past Joe's head like a bee in flight. Taking a more considered aim at his assailant's torso, Joe squeezed off his second shot. The .44-calibre ball was an effective man-stopper and it did just that. Striking the deputy in his belly, its momentum knocked him off balance and he fell heavily on to the unyielding couplings. As a bloody froth bubbled up out of his mouth, he attempted to say something.

Stabbing pains continued to strike at Joe's hand and left him in no mood to offer considerations. Cocking his revolver, he took a cold, calculated aim at the bloodied features below him. That man's eyes spread wide in mortal terror as he contemplated his doom.

Although hardened to killing, Bill felt mild elation at having dispatched Pritchett's deputy with such accomplished ease.

Unfortunately his contentment proved to be short-lived. The sudden reduction in speed took him completely by surprise. Facing the rear of the train, he was jerked backwards and completely lost his footing. Unable to help himself, he fell full length on to the unforgiving iron rails. The back of his head struck solid metal with sickening force. Somehow he instinctively kept hold of his revolver, but all the wind was knocked out of his body. Even in that state, he was aware of a frantic yelling coming from somewhere off to his left. Why couldn't they just hush up? His head swam and he felt bile rising up into his throat. Keeping his eyes closed, he desperately tried to drag some air into his starved lungs.

Gunshots sounded nearby and Bill struggled to make sense of it all. Ignoring the pounding in his skull, he forced open his eyes. It was at that moment that Deke Pritchett appeared over the side of the rails. Discounting Bill's immobile form as presenting no threat, the marshal aimed his Remington revolver directly at Joe's broad back. It was an easy shot, but Pritchett took his time over it. He savoured the pleasure of dispatching such a persistent troublemaker.

Clarity of thought finally returned to Bill. From his prone position he glanced over at Omaha's finest and saw murder in that man's eyes. But he also recalled that they needed him alive. Cursing silently, he levelled his revolver and then pulled to the right. The weapon bucked in his hand and for a brief moment his target was hidden by the vaporous discharge. When it cleared, Marshal Pritchett had quite simply disappeared.

'Oh shit!' exclaimed Bill in dismay. 'Stop the goddamn train!'

81

CHAPTER TEN

Joe, still suffering agonies from the injury to his hand, had twisted around to face the new threat. Catching on immediately, he rushed over to the edge of the rails. He gazed back down the line and spotted the marshal lying on the grass where he had fallen. Turning to face the engine, he bellowed at Barnaby to stop. There was no response. The constant noise in the cab, added to the distance, meant that the engineer just could not hear him. 'Sweet Jesus,' snarled Joe. 'Why's everything got to be so difficult?'

Cocking his revolver, he aimed directly at the smokestack. The first shot caused wild alarm, whilst the second attracted the engineer's rapt attention.

'Back the train up,' hollered Joe, gesticulating wildly.

The message was understood and the brakes were applied. This time the change in motion didn't catch anybody unawares. Bill, now sitting upright, was quite obviously not himself yet, so it was up to the other man to see to business.

'Keep an eye on Pritchett,' commanded Joe. 'I need to check on his deputies.'

Returning to the end of the car, he peered down at his gut-shot victim. He was saved the trouble of administering the *coup de grace*. The man was sprawled lifelessly across the couplings, head hanging down, blood trickling from his nose and mouth. The other reluctant lawman was still 'hanging' around; sheer fatigue meant that he had stopped his yelling. A wry smile broke out on Joe's face, despite the extreme torment that he was suffering. Aiming directly at the luckless character, he called over to him.

'You can either let go or take a bullet. The choice is yours. If it was me I'd jump, because look, we've even stopped the train for you.'

It was true; the train had stopped prior to moving back down the track. Yet even then the man seemed undecided, so Joe discharged a chamber into the air to speed him on his way. The deputy tumbled to the ground like a side of prime beef. As the train began to move again, Joe called out, 'You didn't get to shooting, so I'm letting you walk. Keep clear of this train and follow the tracks to Fremont. You should make it before dark. If I ever see you again, I'll kill you!'

With that salutary remark, he turned away and promptly sat down. He felt light-headed, but couldn't think why until he looked at his left hand. The deceased deputy's ball had completely severed his little finger. Blood was flowing and the pain was abominable. He dragged a kerchief out of a pocket and was attempting to bandage the wound when Bill arrived. As that man took in the scene, genuine concern clouded his face.

'You don't look too good, Joe. Here let me see to that.'

So saying, he tightly bound the kerchief around Joe's hand, so that the wound was at least protected.

'You've lost a mess of blood. Soon as we stop at Fremont, you find a sawbones, you hear?' A sudden recollection of the place triggered in his mind. 'That's if there is one, mind. That place doesn't even qualify as a "one-horse town".'

Mention of that settlement focused Joe's thoughts. He needed to know one thing above all else. 'Where's that goddamned marshal got to?'

'He ain't going anywhere,' replied Bill dismissively. 'The fall knocked seven shades of shit out of him and his shoulder's bleeding some.'

Joe displayed unaccustomed anxiety. 'If he dies, we could be held accountable for this day's work!'

Bill appeared unconcerned by any prospect of account-ability, but nonetheless held his hands up in a conciliatory fashion as he responded. 'Don't you concern yourself about that. I could have paroled him to Jesus, but all he got was a flesh wound. You take a breather, while I go reel him in.'

So saying, he rose up and took his bearings. He momentarily smiled as he spotted the sole surviving deputy rapidly hoofing it away from the train. Clambering over the rails to the other side of the car, Bill looked over the edge. Marshal Pritchett's unhappy figure languished a short way down the track. The train had conveniently reversed just far enough and so he signalled for Barnaby to stop. With the screeching of brakes, the gentle pace quickly fell off until they came to a halt.

Coolly drawing his revolver, Bill called down, 'Slowly, pull that hold-out gun from inside your jacket and toss it on the grass. You make any little move that I don't like and I'll pop a cap.'

The fight seemed to have temporarily left the lawman, because he complied immediately and then sat brooding quietly whilst his captor clambered down from the flat car. He found his reversal of fortune very hard to stomach. By failing to gain the upper hand, he had effectively delivered himself into Wakefield's hands. His future prospects were looking bleak. Then again, he wasn't in federal hands just yet. . . .

Bill's boots kicked up dust as he strolled over. He picked up the hideaway gun first and then made a short detour to recover Pritchett's Remington. No longer benefiting from the breeze on a moving train, the exertion caused him to break sweat. The weather had been unremittingly hot and dry; it wasn't just the locomotive that needed water. There was a raw, desolate feeling to their surroundings that could surely get to a man. The lack of motion emphasized just how much the train and its occupants were completely isolated. An unreal peace had fallen, broken only by the occasional emission of steam from the remote engine.

The two men regarded each other in silence for a moment, before Pritchett spat out accusingly, 'First you're working for me, then you're not. You're awful hard to get a handle on, Hickok!'

That man's eyes glinted dangerously as he replied. 'You had no call to butcher that nice kid in the hotel. He was no threat to you.'

'He could squeeze a trigger, couldn't he? Anyhoo, since when did you get so squeamish? You've killed everything that walks or crawls.'

A shadow passed over Bill's features, which entirely failed to soften them. 'Maybe I've seen the error of my ways, or maybe I just took a liking to him. None of which matters a hill of beans to you. Just mark my words. If you speak of this to Wakefield, I'll put another ball in you. He needs you alive, so I'll just hobble you for life. Savvy?'

Before Pritchett could answer, a voice cut in from the

stack of rails behind them. Joe had been observing their parley with some disquiet. He would have given anything to know what had passed between them and had decided to break up their discourse. 'Put him in the passenger car, Bill. See if you can bind his wound. I'll join you afore long.'

With that he turned away. If the two of them really wanted to talk, there was not a damn thing he could do about it, but the implications of that gnawed on him real bad.

Barnaby Jones was sick and tired of the young man's bellyaching. He could quite understand why somebody would want to bust his face up, because he was tempted to add to the damage himself. By way of escape, he had even contemplated attempting to get the rogue rail back in line on the sixth car, but common sense won out. Far better to get help at Fremont, than risk losing some fingers. The sooner they got moving again the better. Then he could put Toby back to work and shut him up.

So it was that the engineer welcomed Joe's arrival. He watched as that man clambered up on to the tender to retrieve his long rifle. He seemed to be favouring his left hand, the reason becoming obvious as he returned to the cab. After establishing the motive behind the sudden braking earlier, Joe got down to business.

'As soon as I get back to the rear, I want you to get going at your best speed for Fremont. It shouldn't take long, even moving slowly.' Without waiting on Barnaby's response, Joe then rounded fiercely on Toby. 'When we arrive, don't even think about skipping off. We're holding Pritchett back there and he's just aching for a piece of you. You see, someone's told him that you're going to testify against him in a federal court.'

Toby turned very pale as he digested this fact. He was beginning to wonder just what he had done to deserve such a turn of events. 'All I did was pocket a few bucks on the side, mister. If I hadn't agreed to it, the marshal would have beaten me to a pulp.'

Joe actually felt some sympathy for the clerk's plight, but couldn't afford to display it. 'All you have to do is tell that to the federal marshal. It might not even come to that. Once Pritchett knows for definite that he's trapped, he'll probably tell me what I need to know.'

With that, Joe dropped down from the cab and made his way to the rear of the train.

Bill had bound his prisoner's flesh wound with a sleeve from the injured man's own shirt by the time Joe returned. The ball had passed on, leaving a clean gash, but that was undoubtedly painful and had left Pritchett looking pale and out of sorts. The big man was attempting to find comfort on a hard slatted bench seat but with little success.

Joe gratefully sat down, just as the train started moving again. His left hand was aching abominably and he would have gladly exchanged a week's pay for a bottle of laudanum. Pritchett glanced over at him peevishly. 'Just where the hell are you taking me, Wakefield?'

Joe did not really feel like getting into conversation with him, but was willing to do anything that might help to take his mind off the permanent discomfort.

'We're taking on water at Fremont and then heading full chisel for the railhead. Unless you want to give me a name. Do that and you can get off whenever you want.'

Both he and Bill were watching the corrupt lawman closely. Mention of the railhead brought about a startling change in his demeanour. For the first time, they saw real fear etched on his face. 'Why there?' he demanded. 'There's no federal officer anywhere near Grand Island.'

'No,' responded Joe, 'but it is full of armed tracklayers, who couldn't give two bits for a big city marshal or anybody who just might could want to rescue him.'

However logical that answer was, it cut no ice with Pritchett. He was plainly rattled.

'I've got spondulix, see? More than you can shake a stick at. Set me down in Fremont and you'll both be able to live high on the hog.'

There was a pleading note to his voice that set his two captors to thinking. It was Joe who narrowly arrived at a possible reason first. 'You're riding on a supply train and we *all* know what's been happening to them, don't we, you son of a bitch!'

Pritchett stared at him in silence, apparently mesmerized. He began to lick his lips, as though suddenly in desperate need for the Lone Pine tobacco that he habitually chewed. Beads of sweat formed on his forehead and he began to rub a pair of very clammy hands together.

Bill began to lose patience. 'Tell us where they're going to lift the rails or I'll set to work on that wound.'

The unhappy lawman stared at him with undisguised hatred, but remained silent. He was a hard man and no stranger to pain, but tolerance to casual torture is far different than actually dying and Joe suddenly had the answer. 'Very well. Once the engineer's taken on water, we'll truss you up like a turkey in the cab, open the throttle and leave you to it. How's that sound?'

'You wouldn't dare,' Pritchett responded hesitantly. 'The Union Pacific would hang you out to dry if you deliberately smashed up one of their trains.'

'If we don't know where the ambush is, it'll be wrecked

88

anyhoo,' Joe threw back. 'Only this way, you go with it.'

'You're a madman!' yelled Pritchett, manically rocking back and forth on his bench seat.

Joe shook his head slowly. 'No, I'm a man who aims to see this through, is all.'

The two men stared fixedly at each other for what seemed like an age, before Pritchett finally buckled. 'Just this side of Columbus. About three miles out.'

Joe needed to be sure. 'They derail the train and kill everyone on it?'

The marshal looked away before answering. 'Just as before. Those are their orders.'

'Well, that's just dandy,' muttered Bill. 'Out of the frying pan and into the fire.'

The two men stood on the open-air platform at the back of the passenger car. Joe had his left hand cradled against his chest in an attempt to relieve the pain. He had made up his mind on the action to be taken. The problem was that the outcome of his plan depended totally on Bill's commitment towards it. Keeping his voice low, he outlined his intentions. 'While we're taking on water in Fremont, we telegraph ahead to Columbus and instruct that gang of cut-throats to carry out the derailment on the far side of the town instead. When we arrive there, you collect your horse from the livery and ride out after them ahead of us. Stop them from lifting the track and keep them busy until I can get there on the train. Then we'll have them between a rock and a hard place.'

'You've got it all thought out, haven't you? Except for the part where I take a bullet.' It was obvious that Bill wasn't completely sold on the idea. 'How come I drew the short straw?'

'Because you've got the horse and I've got the wound.

I'm not going to bleed to death, but it's enough to slow me down. Besides, it's what you signed on for.'

A blast on the steam whistle announced their arrival in Fremont. The afternoon was well advanced. It seemed to have taken an age to travel the thirty or so miles from Omaha, but once the locomotive had taken on water all would be different. Whilst that was happening they had time to see to business. The so-called town was little more than a few shacks and had only been in existence for some ten years. Strangely, it had been named after the famous explorer General John Charles Fremont, who was still living and therefore not really deserving of such an honour. It boasted a water tower, cookhouse and telegraph office, but little else.

'Who's in charge of your gang of thugs?'

A tightly bound Deke Pritchett glanced up sullenly at Joe's peremptory demand. He seemed little inclined to co-operate, but then had an apparent change of heart. 'Slattery. Brett Slattery and you'll have your hands full with him, sonny boy! Just see if you don't. He's what they call "double tough" in these parts. Ha ha!'

Leaving him in the passenger car, Joe and Bill collected Toby from the cab. Engineer Jones was happy to be rid of his unwilling assistant for a while. The young man was smut-stained and weary, which combined with his earlier injuries to give him the look of a squalid vagrant, but he possessed a particular skill that they needed.

Reaching the telegraph office, Joe presented the operator with a handwritten message that he required sending to a certain Brett Slattery in Columbus. Its author was supposedly Marshal Deke Pritchett, who just happened to be making a brief visit to Fremont. With the clerk tapping away on the telegraph key, Joe instructed Toby to translate. As the stilted oratory progressed, Bill realized the reason behind it and nodded his head approvingly. Because they didn't know just whom they could trust, Joe was using Toby to check the operator's work. Without knowing in advance what was on the message, the Omaha operator couldn't play them false, either. It was all very clever. The more Bill saw of Joe Wakefield, the better he liked and respected him.

With their bit of duplicity complete, the trio visited the railroad cookhouse. It was shaping up to be a long night and they all needed food. Buffalo steaks, beans and boiling hot coffee answered their needs perfectly. Toby's delivery of a large plate of the same for Barnaby at least guaranteed him a civil reception. The engineer had insisted on remaining with the train in order to supervise the securing of the loose rails. As the other two men strolled back to the passenger car, Joe inevitably had a question.

'Have you heard of this Brett Slattery, Bill?'

'Oh yeah,' replied that man. 'He's a born killer and mean as they come.'

'Meaner than you?'

'That'll be the day!'

Bretton Horace Slattery stared hard at the telegraph operator's rapid scrawl. He was the only one of his motley crew who possessed knowledge of both ciphers and letters. It gave him a certain status; that and his lethal ability with any kind of weapon. The five men were gathered around a grubby table in the town's only saloon. The establishment's other occupants well knew to give them a wide berth.

'What's amiss, Brett?' demanded one of the others impatiently. 'Three miles this side or three miles that side makes no odds to us. Let's just do it!'

'If you had more than just hammered shit for brains, Dunc, you'd realize that this doesn't read right. Why change the plan?'

The big man glared at the others as though expecting a reply, although they all knew that none would be forthcoming. The livid scar under his right eye seemed to endow him with an air of frightening menace that left silence as the best option.

'If it looks wrong, then it is wrong,' announced Brett decisively. 'That poxy law dog's got something on his mind.'

Dunc tried again. 'So ain't we gonna do the job?'

'It's a Yankee train, isn't it?' snarled their leader softly. 'Of course we're going to wreck it. But we'll do it where I want to.'

He rose to his feet. The matter was closed. The huge LeMat revolver protruding from his belt only seemed to emphasize his power over the other men. As far as they were concerned, he could lift the rails anywhere that he goddamned pleased!

CHAPTER ELEVEN

The sun was losing its power by the time the train arrived at Columbus. For the last five miles of the journey Barnaby had kept the speed down, so that any sabotage could be spotted in time. For him it was sweaty, nerve-wracking work, but the absence of trouble proved that Joe's telegraph had worked.

The town that they were so grateful to reach had been founded in 1856 on land that at that time still tenuously belonged to the Pawnee Indians. Those unfortunates surrendered their rights to it a year later. The White Eyes so desired it because of its location on the proposed route of the transcontinental railroad. That had now arrived, but as so often happened, change had brought trouble with it.

Whilst the engineer took on yet more water, the two railroad detectives left the Union Pacific depot to visit the saloon. One man stood as much chance of obtaining information as two, so Joe bought a bottle of the local bug juice and took it outside. In the absence of a sawbones it was the closest that he was going to get to some doctoring. He found a quiet corner and with a heartfelt sigh dropped gratefully to the ground. It was going to hurt powerful bad. Grimacing, he removed the makeshift bandage and peered down at his damaged hand. It was raw, bloody and throbbing intolerably. Extracting the cork with his teeth, Joe held his hand out and looked away. As the raw spirit washed over the wound, he howled uncontrollably. His ear-splitting display attracted little attention. The frontier was used to odd behaviour.

Although not normally a drinking man, he took a long swig from the bottle. As the fiery liquid hit his stomach, the pain eased slightly. Feeling uncharacteristically sorry for himself, he wondered whether perhaps it was a good time to get stinking drunk.

'Some say you need plenty of that before a fight, but I don't subscribe.'

Joe looked up to see Bill regarding him sympathetically. 'Well, pardon me all to hell,' he responded. 'Here, help yourself.'

His companion hunkered down next to him and accepted the bottle. 'Maybe just one to cut through the dust before I get to riding.'

Joe stared at him expectantly. 'What have you heard?'

'The barkeep's not partial to Slattery's ways. He's the sort of customer who frightens away the regulars. Apparently he and his crew left this pisspit not long ago. They were heading south-west, which sounds about right.'

After taking a second generous swig of whiskey, Bill plonked the bottle down in the dust with a definite air of satisfaction. 'Can't ever see those temperance drinks catching on,' he remarked genially. 'Somehow seems like they're missing the point.' Then, picking up the soiled bandage, he gently fastened it around Joe's infinitely tender hand.

'I'm going to get my horse from the livery,' he announced. 'Wish me luck. And if you should perceive gunplay out there, you just come running, you hear?'

With that, Bill turned away and made for the livery stables. He had left his horse there before his chance meeting with Joe and Dan on the train to Omaha. It was hard to credit that that had only been the previous day. As Joe watched the other man stride away, a sudden chill swept over him. Just what if that hadn't been a coincidence? By his actions, Bill had shown himself to be an apparently loyal employee, but a single day was not long to know a man.

Reluctantly, Joe hauled himself to his feet, the bottle of rotgut completely forgotten. Loosening the revolver in its holster, he followed on to the stables. He really didn't know what he thought to discover. It was just instinct that pulled him along in Bill's wake.

Reaching the main entrance, Joe stopped and drew in a deep breath. His hand was aching abominably. He felt like shit and genuinely hoped that this time nothing would come from following a hunch. From inside, he could hear Bill greeting his horse like a long-lost friend. Slipping into the large building, Joe was just in time to see that man heave his saddle up on to the waiting animal. And then he saw it!

The unmistakeable shape of a Sharps rifle protruded from a leather flap. That potent weapon, in the hands of a man wearing a duster coat, had very possibly taken Jake's life three days earlier. The fact that Bill had chosen to leave such a valuable possession in the stable compounded the probability. Anger suddenly coursed through his veins as Joe realized just what a fool he had been. The pain in his damaged hand was abruptly forgotten. Drawing and cocking his Colt Army, he barked out one word. 'Hickok!'

That man froze in the act of fastening the girth strap.

His measured response came almost instantaneously. 'I thought my friends called me Bill,' he stated calmly without turning. 'You are still my friend, aren't you?'

God, but he was a cool customer. Joe advanced slowly, his weapon pointed unwaveringly at the other man's back. 'Step away from that horse and keep your hands where I can see them.'

Bill did as instructed.

'Now, turn around, so that I can see what an assassin looks like.'

Again Bill complied. His face was a blank mask, as though any anger or surprise that he may have been feeling just did not exist. Their hard, probing eyes met in the manner of two suspicious men who have just encountered each other for the first time. Joe had an uncomfortable feeling that he wasn't really in control of the situation, even though he was the one holding a gun.

Keeping his hands well away from his sides, Bill opened his mouth as though to speak and suddenly emitted a strange clicking sound. The great beast at his side lunged forward from a standing start. The unsecured saddle careered off its back as it charged towards Joe. It was all he could do to leap out of its path. Falling sideways, he banged his left hand and was immediately assailed by a wave of nausea. Before he could react, Bill had seized his right hand and wrenched the revolver out of his weakened grasp.

Sprawled helplessly on the hard-packed earth, Joe found himself gazing up into the muzzle of his own weapon. The moustachioed face behind it was no longer impassive. It wore a broad smile, which contained no hint of malice.

'I hope you haven't got that wound bleeding again,

Josiah Wakefield. Only you really shouldn't sneak up on a man like that.'

For all that his tone was friendly, the muzzle remained pointing directly at Joe's forehead. Yet if Hickok really wanted him dead, it would already have happened, so he decided to push his luck a bit.

'Three days ago you killed my prisoner!' It was a statement rather than a question and the other man chose to treat it as such.

'Oh, I killed Jake, all right. It was a doosey of a shot and I enjoyed it. Believe me when I tell you that he needed killing.'

'So who are you working for?'

Bill sighed and slowly shook his head. He supposed that if ever there was a time to swear on his mother's life and tell the truth, then this was it. 'I was down on my luck and in need of a grubstake. Deke Pritchett offered me a job. The man's an asshole, but needs must and I accepted. I was to keep an eye on Jake and his crew in case anything went wrong. That poxy lawman didn't want any shit heading back his way. I'd seen how good you were with a long gun, so after dropping Jake I cut and ran. It was complete coincidence that I got on that particular train at Columbus to report back to Pritchett, but you know what? I got to liking the two of you. So I decided to work for you instead and as of now, *you* owe me ten dollars American.'

Despite the situation, Joe couldn't stop himself from chuckling. The barefaced cheek of the man was quite remarkable.

'So if you're quite finished sneaking and skulking,' Bill continued, 'I need to make tracks, else we'll miss the party.'

With that, he oh so slowly lowered the hammer on the

97

Colt Army, reversed the butt and handed it back to its owner. Joe accepted it with mixed feelings. He had been easily bested, which did not sit well; and yet he was finally quite convinced that Bill Hickok was telling the truth. Ruefully holstering his weapon, he clambered to his feet and offered his good right hand. As the other man accepted it, Joe remarked, 'Be careful out there. They'll have the advantage of numbers.'

'That's all they'll have,' returned Bill with a confident grin.

Joe watched as the other man saddled up and then mounted. 'That's quite a horse you've got there,' he remarked with genuine admiration.

'Ain't that the truth,' Bill responded as he stirred the animal into motion. Then, with a brief wave, he was off. Heading south-west on the trail of five very desperate men.

Brett Slattery sat his horse and minutely surveyed their surroundings, completely ignoring his four men as they toiled away with heavy crowbars. Their intention was to entirely remove two parallel rails, but, with one exception, they were woefully unused to hard labour. Three of them were sweating profusely and threw envious glances at their companion, Jase Decker. His powerful, well-defined muscles were a product of a lengthy spell working for the Union Pacific Railroad as a grader. Tiring of the relentless toil, he had chosen instead to throw in his lot with Slattery.

'There ain't nobody out there, Brett,' whined a scrawny, pocked-marked individual named Clayton. 'Why don't you lend a hand, shifting these tarnal rails?'

The exertion must have loosened his wits, because he would not normally have dared to venture such a proposal. As it was, Slattery affected to ignore him for a few moments, before abruptly reining his horse around. Drawing a huge knife from a scabbard on his saddle, he settled his cold eyes on the suddenly very nervous Clayton.

'If you make any more fool suggestions, I'll carve my initials on your tits with this Arkansas toothpick. You'll carry my mark on you for the rest of your days, savvy?'

The other man paled considerably in response to such a graphic threat. All those present knew that Slattery would carry it out, as the infliction of pain on others was something of a pastime of his.

'I'm powerful sorry, Brett,' Clayton stammered anxiously. 'I didn't mean nothing by it. All this hard work's got me riled up, is all.'

Slattery grunted and turned away, but he wasn't finished. 'Something's just not hunky dory about this set-up. I can feel it in my water. So while you muttonheads work those spikes loose, I'm going to keep my eyes peeled for anything that doesn't look right.'

He also decided that he made too good a target, sitting high up on his lonesome. So he dismounted and slowly prowled around his horse, never staying still for long and never straying far. Such behaviour illustrated how Slattery had managed to stay alive when so many had attempted to put him in a cold hole in the ground.

Josiah Wakefield clambered up into the passenger car to check that their prisoner was still securely bound. Pritchett favoured him with a sour look. 'Christ, Wakefield, I'm starving. There must be a cookhouse in this burgh. If you're going to shoot a man, you might at least feed him.'

'I wasn't the one that shot you and besides, you shouldn't wreck the Union Pacific's trains if you want to eat their food,' Joe flippantly replied.

On that note, he left the car, pursued by a torrent of abuse, and headed up the track. With mortal danger imminent, Joe had decided to ride in the cab. That's where the firepower would be needed and to that end he had Pritchett's revolvers tucked into his belt. His mind was a seething mass of anxiety, mainly due to action taken at the final stop that he had made after watching Hickok ride off. On the spur of the moment, he had sent off a strangely worded telegram to Colonel Thomas Cartwright at the railhead. It read as follows:

APPREHENDED MAN BEHIND TRAIN WRECKING STOP HE HAS TOLD ME EVERYTHING STOP BRINGING HIM TO RAILHEAD STOP REQUIRE THAT YOU SUMMON FEDERAL MARSHAL STOP.

He had no idea just how many men would read that message, but he fully expected the inclusion of 'he has told me everything' to stir some dust. It could also have brought even more trouble down on their heads!

If he hadn't been engaged in a deadly manhunt, Bill would have enjoyed his evening ride over the prairie. The glare and heat from the sun had dissipated, which should make finding his prey that much easier. If they were where they were supposed to be! It felt good to be back in the saddle and away from the towns. It was such a shame that they happened to be where all the money was. To him they all seemed to smell of sweat and human waste.

Ownership of a Sharps rifle was not the only thing that he had in common with Joe. He also possessed a drawtube spyglass. Carefully, he scrutinized the track and the land bordering it for any sign of life. 'Damn it!' he cursed. Couldn't that back-shooting bastard read a telegram properly?

He gently urged his mount forward. There was nothing for it but to keep advancing slowly, until either he found Slattery and his gang of degenerates or the train arrived.

The two rails had finally been lifted and heaved to one side. With the hard work completed, the four men's spirits had started to pick up. Ahead of them lay the prospect of some entertaining carnage, followed by the possibility of a little risk-free bloodshed *and* looting. So why was it that their leader remained so resolutely morose?

Decker, all sinew and muscle, was less in awe of Slattery than the others. Hefting a heavy crowbar easily in his hands, he asked, 'Why not lighten up, Brett? You're acting like a porch baby. The hard work's done on this job and if there was anyone out there we'd see them coming.'

Slattery eyed him sourly. At any other time that man's presumption would have ended badly, but instead he merely replied, 'Feller I know could bring a man down *before* you even saw him. You'd be crow bait before you even got wind.'

Their stalker had travelled a further two miles or so before movement finally registered through his spyglass. Grunting with satisfaction, Bill dismounted and, leading his animal, moved slowly forward, all the while contemplating his limited options. Because the terrain was so flat and open it would be very hard to sneak up on those murderous sons of bitches. This, and the disparity in numbers, meant that he would have to open fire at long range. If he could inflict casualties and keep them pinned down until his current employer arrived, things could just maybe work out. *And* it all had to be done before the best of the light drained out of the sky.

Mind made up, he halted and ground-tethered his horse with a pilfered cavalry picket pin. With his glass, he carefully checked his surroundings to ensure that he hadn't blundered into a trap. Only then did he concentrate on the little group ahead. Slattery's brutal visage swam into view. Bill was very aware that it would behove him to drop that man first, but by constantly moving around his horse the wrecker's leader was cunningly making such a result nigh on impossible. Bill didn't recognize any of the others, so with no priorities it became a case of taking the easiest shot.

He had deliberately left his Sharps unloaded whilst in Columbus, so that the powder did not deteriorate. Dropping the falling block, he loaded a linen cartridge. Then came a percussion cap, followed by a careful adjustment of the ladder sight. And since it was always blustery on the plains, allowance for windage had great relevance. Finally all was ready. It was a long shot, easily four hundred yards, but by using his own loads the marksman knew that his weapon possessed the necessary power.

Tucking the butt tightly into his shoulder, Bill lined up on a broad back and squeezed the first trigger. He had deliberately moved slowly, so that his heart rate was steady. Breathing in and then slowly out, the manhunter squeezed again. As usual with black powder, his view was temporarily obscured – but it mattered little. Just like Joe Wakefield, he had hunted both man and beast and so knew instinctively when he had made a kill.

Jase Decker coughed up a gout of blood as an unstoppable

force threw him forward. He had struck the ground before his surprised cronies could react.

'I knew it,' bellowed Slattery as he hit the dirt next to Decker's twitching body. 'It's a set-up.' He alone had his Spencer Carbine pointed in the right direction, but it served little purpose at such range. 'Keep your goddamned heads down. If that cockchafer can't see us, he can't shoot us.'

Bill searched for another victim but to no avail. Short of becoming a horse killer, all he could do was bide his time. Twice more he fired, mainly for effect. He struck no one, but did succeed in preventing their escape. The sudden violence also scared away the untethered horses and so separated Slattery's crew from their spare ammunition. Bill, having fulfilled his part of the plan, was now in need of reinforcements. And then, as though by divine intervention, he heard it! The unmistakeable chuffa-chuffa-chuffa sound of a modern miracle: the steam engine. Slattery and his men were close to the tracks and would fall easy prey to Joe's rifle in that man's elevated position. The gang of cut-throats would have no choice other than to make a forced move.

The last two miles were covered at a snail's pace. Joe was impatient to push on, but the engineer would have none of it. Somewhere up ahead, the rails were lifted and Barnaby Jones had no intention of speeding to his death. Even in the noisy cab, the three men heard the distant report of a high-powered rifle. Toby dropped into a crouch and earned a reprimand from the engineer. 'Keep feeding that firebox. Nobody told you to stop, goddammit!'

The words were barely out of his mouth when he spotted the section of denuded crossties up ahead. Bellowing out a warning, he heaved on the brake lever. Joe was swiftly by his side. He had just made his own discovery and was about to add to Barnaby's troubles.

'I know you didn't sign on to fight,' he shouted over the din of screeching metal, 'but trouble has found us now.' With that, he handed Pritchett's Remington revolver to the unhappy engineer. 'Do you know how to use one of these?'

'Cock, aim and fire,' Barnaby threw back dismissively. 'How hard can that be?'

As the completely undamaged train ground to a halt some fifty yards away, Slattery knew immediately what they had to do. To remain there was to invite annihilation. Their only chance was to rush the cab. If they could get up close with that, then the distant sharpshooter would be severely restricted. Glaring at his little group, he remarked, 'When I say, get on your feet and take that engine. One, two, three, go!'

On board the stationary train, the now redundant Toby jumped with shock as he suddenly saw four armed men rushing for the cab. At the sight of the vicious desperados, sheer terror overwhelmed him. It would have made little difference had he been armed, as it takes a certain kind of man to pull a trigger in anger. Strangely, instead of leaping from the cab and running like hell, he chose to clamber up on to the tender. There he began to heave logs out of the way, as though trying to burrow down to safety.

Dismissing the clerk's strange antics from his mind, Joe awkwardly balanced the barrel of his Sharps on his damaged left hand. The weight felt almost insupportable. There was no time to individually assess the likely capabilities of the men approaching them. Rapidly aiming at a cadaverous figure in the lead, he squeezed both triggers. In the comparatively enclosed space, the roar was deafening. The barrel jumped in his hand, so inducing a fresh wave of pain, and he found himself enveloped in a sulphurous cloud. Assailed by nausea, he stepped back and stumbled in the unfamiliar surroundings. Falling to the floor, he felt weak and in no all-fired hurry to get back on his feet. He really should have drawn his revolver, but instead made a feeble attempt to reload his rifle.

The heavy ball smashed into the man known as Clayton and threw him back on to the ground. Such was the overwhelming force of the blow that he never even uttered a sound. Whether dead or alive, he was definitely out of the battle and his sudden demise galvanized his cronies.

Slattery fired and levered his Spencer on the run. 'Lay down some fire or they'll have us all,' he bellowed harshly at his two remaining men. Their projectiles began to slam into the side of the wooden cab, which had the apparent effect of suppressing any return fire. His breathing was laboured from the unaccustomed exercise, but he was nearly there. Then, without a word to his companions, their supposed leader suddenly veered off to his right. His course took him around the front of the great hissing machine and on to the other side of the cab.

Barnaby had never been in a gunfight before, but he wasn't going to let that stop him. Cocking the unfamiliar weapon, he fired over the top of the thick wooden panelling. With a comforting roar, the revolver bucked in his hand. Emboldened, he cocked and fired again. It never occurred to him that there might not be anyone in front of his gun muzzle. About to fire a third time, he was suddenly aware of a movement by the entrance. Instinctively pulling back towards the firebox, his horrified gaze focused on the revolver aimed directly at him. In that split second before death, there was nothing to be said or considered.

Dunc's brutalized face above and behind the weapon creased into a venomous smile as a prelude to squeezing the trigger. To him, there could be no greater pleasure than the almost sexual anticipation of a kill. By way of climax, he contracted his forefinger. The hammer dropped on to the small copper cap beneath and there was … nothing. Misfire!

Barnaby's eyes flickered with disbelief and he felt a sudden unexpected warmth as liquid flowed down his left leg. Shame at such a reaction and incandescent rage at its cause propelled him into action. He aimed directly at Dunc's horrified figure and with manic intensity discharged four more chambers. After the first shot he couldn't see anything but acrid smoke. In spite of the point-blank range only one ball struck flesh and bone, but it was enough. The gory headshot snuffed the man's life out in an instant and left him in an untidy heap by the side of the train that he had intended to destroy.

Barnaby was temporarily beyond all reason. He continued to squeeze the trigger, so that the Remington repeatedly dry-fired. Dunc's sole remaining accomplice was hardened to gunplay and therefore unimpressed by such an empty threat. The man was level with the floor of the cab and swung inward to snap off a quick shot. He held a massive relic of the Mexican War, a Colt Walker that was really only suitable to be carried in a saddle holster. If only one ball from that monster had struck Barnaby, the beleaguered train would have been stranded for the duration.

Joe was on his knees and had temporarily abandoned his rifle. Even as Dunc's ill-favoured features were destroyed, he drew and cocked his single-action Colt. So when the next assailant appeared in the entrance, he simply leaned forward and placed the gun muzzle up against the man's greasy head. The detonation blew blood and brain matter out on to the prairie and left the air tainted with the smell of burnt flesh and hair.

Despite the pain and carnage, Joe's mind was sufficiently clear to have kept a tally. He knew that there was one more wrecker unaccounted for. He also knew that that man was likely to be the most dangerous of them all. On a sudden impulse, he clambered forward and dropped down out of the locomotive. The engineer would just have to take his chances. The two disfigured corpses presented no danger, but as ever he took the time to survey his surroundings. The only man left alive proved to be Bill Hickok, who was walking cautiously towards the train, leading his horse. Without a word, Joe raised his right forefinger and indicated that he was going in pursuit.

Brett Slattery had silently made his way around the engine. Repeated gunshots sounded from inside the cab and instinctively he knew that things were not going well. Unfortunately he had no obvious escape route and so could only rely upon ruthless aggression. Had he only known it, his immediate employer was trussed up in the rear carriage and would have made a useful ally. Such were the fortunes of men in his profession!

Placing his Spencer carefully on the ground, Slattery drew the huge LeMat revolver from his belt. He had taken the gun from a mortally wounded Confederate officer, who no longer had any use for it and who would in any case have wanted his loyal sergeant to slaughter more Yankee invaders with it. At close quarters it was quite the most lethal weapon that he had encountered. A nine-chambered cylinder revolved around a central sixteen-gauge smooth-bore barrel that contained a charge of grapeshot. By cunning use of a lever on the end of the hammer, it was this latter option that he now chose.

The firing had apparently stopped, so Slattery eased up to the cab's entrance. Climbing two steps, he cautiously peered into its interior. Barnaby had slumped to the floor in shock, brought on by his first action. Although the revolver that lay by his side was empty, Slattery could not know that. For the second time that day a monstrous weapon was levelled at the unfortunate engineer. As a forefinger tightened on the trigger, there was unexpected movement on the tender. A displaced log registered in Slattery's peripheral vision as it tumbled off the pile and he twisted to his right.

Toby yelped in alarm at his sudden discovery and thrust his empty hands forward in supplication. His gesture was futile. Slattery saw only a partially concealed figure high up on the tender and immediately fired the shotgun barrel. There was a deafening report, coupled with a huge quantity of smoke. The full charge of scrap iron caught the young telegraph clerk squarely in the chest. Copious amounts of blood splashed over the logs as his torso was thrown back against the woodpile. His broken body slowly slid sideways as though reluctantly acknowledging that its existence was finally over. He had died without a sound.

Slattery climbed up into the cab, advanced on Barnaby and kicked the Remington away from him. He had adjusted his weapon so that the hammer was now directly above one of nine chambers containing .42-calibre balls. The engineer was facing imminent death, until Slattery suddenly had a far better idea. He kicked his prisoner hard in the ribs to ensure that he had his full attention.

'Get on your feet, goddammit. You're going to get this machine moving, back down the track to Columbus.'

Before the startled engineer had time to reply, he found himself very painfully dragged off the floor by his hair. The muzzle of the LeMat was rammed into his neck and he appeared to have no choice other than to comply. It was at that point that Joe Wakefield announced his presence. 'Lower the hammer *very* slowly and place that cannon on the floor.'

Both men froze in their deadly embrace. Mere seconds seemed like a lifetime, but finally Slattery made a move. Very gradually, he cranked his head to the left and looked down at the Colt Army revolver pointed directly at him. The ghost of a grim smile appeared on his face, causing the scar under his right eye to crease in a most unpleasant manner. 'Looks like we've got us a stand-off. If you drop that hammer, this son of a bitch gets it. And my guess is that without him you're stranded.'

Joe involuntarily licked his lips. The big man appeared to have the right of it and that fact gave him no comfort whatsoever. Then movement registered directly opposite him and Bill Hickok leapt up into the cab with all the agility of a mountain lion.

'Hello, Brett,' remarked that individual with studied nonchalance. Both arms hung loosely at his sides. The pistol fighter's posture was completely unthreatening and yet there was no disguising the two fully cocked Colt Navys in his hands. They imbued him with a latent menace that the other man couldn't fail to observe, and so it proved.

The remaining wrecker noticeably paled as he twisted round to face the newcomer. 'You,' he grunted through gritted teeth. His knuckles showed white as he manically gripped the butt of his heavy revolver. Barnaby began to struggle against the pressure of the LeMat, until Slattery swiftly brought his knee up into the man's mid-section. The engineer slumped slightly, but the gun muzzle never left his neck.

'Lower that piece or face the consequences,' Bill commanded.

'Four-dollar words don't cut it with me, Hickok,' responded Slattery harshly. 'You try any fancy moves with those Colts and see where it gets you.'

Those prophetic words were barely out of his mouth before Bill indeed made his move. His right-hand revolver leapt up to the horizontal and flame belched from its muzzle. The .36-calibre ball struck Slattery in the throat and exited from the back of his neck. That man's eyes briefly registered a mixture of disbelief and shock before all life left them. Then his revolver slipped from nerveless fingers and he collapsed on to the floor of the cab. With a theatrical flourish Bill twirled his revolver before returning it to its holster. Only someone with supreme self-confidence in his abilities could have attempted such a bold stroke.

Barnaby had recovered his wind and was staring at his rescuer with stunned amazement. Spots of Slattery's blood coated his face, but he seemed oblivious to it. 'Hot dang, mister,' he proclaimed with genuine astonishment. 'That took some nerve. What if you'd missed?'

'The thought never occurred to me,' Bill responded calmly.

Joe climbed up into the cab and scrutinized the dead man. 'Did you know him?' he asked with frank curiosity.

'Some,' Bill allowed pensively. 'Back in the day.'

It was only then that the two men noticed the other broken body pathetically sprawled across the logs in the tender.

'Oh shit!' exclaimed Joe. 'Looks like we did good, but they did better.'

CHAPTER TWELVE

Lieutenant Colonel Thomas Cartwright, formerly of the Army of the Potomac, read Joe Wakefield's telegraph for the third or maybe even the fourth time. It was the sentence, 'HE HAS TOLD ME EVERYTHING STOP' that was particularly exercising his mind. Was it deliberately ambiguous, or did it merely appear so because the Union Pacific's newly appointed employee had been under great stress when he wrote it? Or, was the sharpshooter and buffalo-hunter-turned-railroad-detective a good deal smarter than anybody might have reasonably expected? One thing was for sure: he had certainly shown an aptitude for survival.

Cartwright's stained teeth worked hard on the fat cigar that befitted his exalted position as track boss. He himself was under a great deal more stress than anybody could possibly have comprehended. The colonel was charged with advancing the railhead at the fastest possible pace. Yet, because of his own particular pact with the Devil, it was also in his own interests to progress as slowly as possible, so long as it was not apparent to his official employers. Hence the sudden onset of some very bloody and very mysterious train-wrecking. And, so as to appear that he was doing everything within his power to stop them, he had even cunningly resorted to employing someone to investigate them. What he hadn't expected was for that individual to be so capable or so persistent.

There was a massive financial incentive for all this mayhem that, if made public, could quite possibly bring down President Andrew Johnson's administration. Certain powerful interests back East stood to make vast sums of money by buying up land before the railroad reached it, but there had been delays in the interminable legal processes. As a result, the dubious speculators needed to slow down, but not completely stop, the progress of the Union Pacific by any means available. It was their good luck that the man with local control just happened to have thwarted ambitions. In the rapidly contracting post-war Union Army, Cartwright would likely have been reduced to first lieutenant and been consigned to some dreary frontier posting. The alternative was to accept a job with the Union Pacific, which had soaked up a large number of demobbed soldiers. That was all very well, but what would become of him when the transcontinental connection was completed? It therefore behoved him to make some real money while he could. All it took was a ruthless disregard for human life. During the recent conflict, he had discovered many times that he had that particular quality.

After careful investigation and consideration he had managed to forge a relationship with the dissolute and corrupt city marshal of Omaha. He had discovered that Deke Pritchett would make the ideal middleman. In that way the colonel was able to distance himself from the actual murder and destruction that had to take place. If, as seemed likely, that fool had got himself apprehended and was now likely to talk, then Cartwright had no choice other than to permanently silence him. The question was, how to achieve that end without attracting suspicion?

He paced up and down the railroad carriage like a caged beast as he weighed up his options. The track boss was proud of his powerful physique and was aware of just how intimidating he could be. Yet this situation called for more than just coercion; it could very well require an unprecedented level of violence.

Mind made up, Cartwright strode to the nearest door and stepped out on to the open-air platform. Dropping down off the carriage, he gazed westward. As far as the eye could see, the route of the Union Pacific stretched before him. The graders had built up the path for the track, but construction was held up by a shortage of rails and crossties. The derailments had drastically affected their delivery and he was being bombarded daily by impatient telegrams from the railroad's chief engineer, General Grenville Dodge, in Chicago.

Catching sight of the walking boss, he bellowed out the man's name and signalled that he should join him. Mike Shaughnessey was the archetypal Irish sergeant. On leaving the Union Army, he had taken his rifle and headed west. His undoubted talents had found a home with the railroad. There was no man better suited to keeping the men working and enforcing discipline. Unfortunately he was also a relatively simple soul, to whom life was either black or white. *And* he was honest. There was no room in his life for any nefarious dealings and so he had been excluded from Cartwright's activities. In fact the only other man at the railhead involved in the murderous campaign was the indispensable telegraph operator, Calum Post.

As the burly Irishman approached, Cartwright gestured

for him to follow on into the carriage. As the door closed behind them, the long room became Cartwright's stage, where he had to work his magic on a man who would be a crucial part of his scheme. Without any preamble, he got straight to the point. 'We've got a problem, Shaughnessey. An almighty big one.'

'You don't have to be telling me, sor,' the other man replied immediately in a thick Irish accent. 'Track-laying's at a standstill. If we don't see a supply train soon, dem graders'll be in Utah and we'll still be sitting here on our bleeding arses!'

Cartwright shook his head impatiently. 'That's nothing compared to what's heading this way. I have been informed by the Pacific Telegraph operator in Columbus that our next supply train has been taken over by a gang of vicious ruffians. They have filled it with blasting powder and intend to attack this railhead.'

Shaughnessey was completely nonplussed by such a development. He gawped at his superior and then ran a meaty hand over his face, as though attempting to massage his wits. Following the maxim of 'hit hard and hit fast', Cartwright continued before the Irishman had time to form a response. 'I want a section of track lifted behind us and a barricade constructed. All the men still have their rifles, so they can man it. And we can't take any chances, so tell them to shoot to kill! It'll be like old times for any Johnny Rebs you've got out there. Those bushwhacking bastards used to enjoy a good ambush.'

All of this was just too much for the hapless Shaughnessey. The prospect of attacking a Union Pacific train quite simply appalled him. 'What if they have prisoners aboard? There's no telling who might get hurt. What if someone's made a mistake and it's not even the same train? It's a hell of a thing you be wanting from me, sor.'

Cartwright moved in close until they were almost face to face. There was an unsettling gleam in his eyes that suggested a myriad of hidden emotions. He reached out and gripped the other man's shoulders. Shaughnessey was a sturdy individual, but he could feel the uncomfortable build-up of pressure.

'There is no mistake. The telegraph was particularly clear and Calum had the Columbus operator repeat it,' Cartwright assured him firmly. 'I am tasked with building this railroad. It will bind the whole country together, so anyone attempting to disrupt it must be dealt with severely. For now, this is an untamed wilderness full of hazards. Innocent people are bound to get hurt along the way, but we will triumph.'

It came to mind that he might be overdoing the patriotic fervour a little, but he needed to bend the walking boss to his will. 'Now *you* go out there and *you* get those men moving. I don't know how much time we've got and if this camp gets destroyed, I won't be the only one to suffer.'

The veiled threat seemed to have an effect, because Shaughnessey suddenly shrugged off Cartwright's grip and squared his shoulders. 'I'll muster the men now, sor. We'll stop anything that comes down that track, but I just hope you've got it right.' Then he repeated his earlier warning, as though that in itself would free him of any subsequent blame. 'It's a terrible thing you be after having me do!'

With that, the former sergeant headed for the carriage door. Apparently he knew his duty, but there was obviously a seed of doubt still lingering in his mind. As the door closed, it occurred to Cartwright that he would have an awful lot of explaining to do in the aftermath, but then it wasn't the first time that he had wrecked the Union Pacific's trains!

Barnaby's big, bluff frame was still trembling with shock. He had spent the war in a protected occupation. This was his first taste of bloody violence and he didn't care for it one bit. His two companions initially eyed him sympathetically, but they soon tired of his melodramatic reaction. They had other things to think on. Toby's shattered body was mute testimony to the fact that their plans were in disarray.

Leaving the engineer to his own private hell, they dropped down out of the cab and contemplated the empty crossties ahead.

'So, what the hell do we do now, *Mister* Wakefield?' Bill Hickok inquired as he gazed quizzically at his employer.

'Looks like we've got some track-laying to do,' remarked Joe without enthusiasm. His hand was throbbing, he felt dead on his feet and he really didn't relish the prospect of lifting two six-hundred-pound rails.

'Then again,' suggested Bill, 'since we no longer have a witness to give to your colonel, we could just steam right back to Columbus and get ourselves a drink. You don't look up to shifting those rails anyhoo.'

'That won't answer,' responded Joe stubbornly. 'Pritchett doesn't know that Toby's kilt. So we get those rails spiked down and head on into the railhead.'

His companion regarded him warily. 'You're a real push-hard, aren't you? And while we're sashaying about on that train, what becomes of my horse? Tell me that.'

Joe wasn't for turning. 'Leave him free to graze. You can

drop off on the way back.'

All that remark succeeded in doing was getting Bill's back up. 'Too thin, my friend. Too thin. I've trusted my life and my possessions to that horse and I'm not just up and leaving him out here in this godforsaken spot. Not for any five dollars a day and found. I'm going to ride him back to the stables in Columbus. You'd be wise to pull this rig back there for the night. Unless you reckon you and that gun-shy engineer can manage those rails between you.'

Instinctively, Joe clutched his injured hand. Damn the man! Bill had him and he knew it. Then again, it occurred to him that arriving at the railhead in the dark was probably a mite too risky. He didn't know what they'd be up against. And by enlisting some tracklayers at the depot, the track could be repaired without a lot of pain and exertion. Finally, there was the simple matter of exhaustion to consider. Since their first confrontation with Marshal Pritchett over breakfast, the two men had been constantly in action and Joe for one was feeling much reduced. His head had been pounding something cruel ever since Bill had tried to knock some sense into him. What he really needed was a good night's rest.

There's stubborn and there's stupid and Joe Wakefield was certainly not the latter, so he bowed to reason. But before they left, he did one thing that the luckless Jake hadn't thought to. With a well-aimed shot, he cut the telegraph wire that ran by the track. That way nobody at the railhead could establish just where the expected supply train had got to and it would likely create a sense of uncertainty in anyone intending them harm.

The rails had been lifted and a sizeable barricade constructed before darkness fell. On Cartwright's instructions, the men had not been told the reason for such unusual activity. There would be time for that later. For now it was sufficient that they had a hot meal. It was likely to be a long night.

There were over one hundred men in camp, so there was no shortage for the task in hand. In addition, there was a large party of track-graders well forward of the rail-head working towards the small town of Kearney, about thirty-five miles to the west. The colonel, confident of his own numbers, had decided to leave them out there. His self-assurance was only slightly dented when he had an urgent visit from Calum Post, the telegraph operator.

'The line's down, Colonel. Somewhere between here and Columbus.'

There could be any number of reasons for such an occurrence and none of them good. What it did do was prove a point to the walking boss.

As the last light drained out of the sky, the two men stood behind the wooden barricade staring east. A man with more sensitivity and imagination might have been tempted to ponder on just what wonders such a vast, untamed country might contain, but Thomas Cartwright was purely driven by greed. With an entirely false gesture of companionship, he placed a hand lightly on Shaughnessey's shoulder.

'You're a good man, Mike. I know you're not happy about all this, but you must see that I haven't any choice. Until the telegraph line is repaired we are cut off. Whoever's on that train doesn't want us summoning help. I believe that this is the next move after wrecking those supply trains. I simply can't ignore it.'

His subordinate had not missed the subtle use of his first name. It was the first time that had ever happened, and Shaughnessey was not so simple that he didn't recognize that it was deliberate. And yet, there had to be something in what the colonel was saying. There was no denying that someone had cut the telegraph and the lack of rails was bringing the track-laying to a standstill. In the flickering light of the wood-and-pitch torches, his honest features contorted with temporary indecision. Then they cleared as he realized that he really didn't have any choice. His loyalties lay with the Union Pacific and that great enterprise was clearly threatened.

'I'm with you, Colonel. Dem bastards out there in the dark have got the first move, so I'll organize the men into shifts. It's after being a very long night!'

CHAPTER THIRTEEN

'Just what the devil are you expecting to find in that camp?'

Bill viewed his employer with barely concealed amazement. That man had just instructed Barnaby to move one of the heavily laden flat cars up beyond the locomotive to form the head of the train and presumably act as some sort of battering ram. It would involve a great deal of careful shunting and decoupling, but was possible because of the existence of a spur line at the Columbus depot.

Joe Wakefield had greeted the new day with renewed vigour. Once again wielding his letter of authorization, he had already sent off a party of workmen on a hand-pumped railroad car to repair the section of track. His left hand was still throbbing unmercifully, but it was now tightly bound with a fresh bandage. His headache had gone and he had wolfed down some steaming coffee, a pan of soup and a can of fruit. Strange breakfast fare indeed, but then he had no idea when he could expect another meal. In the face of Bill's bemused inquiry, he decided to relate the contents of his telegram to Colonel Cartwright.

'This could all be for nothing, in which case all we have wasted is some time. On the other hand. . . .' He left the

121

sentence unfinished. All he had to work on was a hunch, but he was still young enough to place his faith in such things.

Other business had also been taken care of. Toby's blood-soaked body had been removed from the tender under cover of darkness, to await an early burial. In the summer heat it would otherwise soon begin to turn. Deke Pritchett had remained confined to the passenger car, oblivious to the key witness's demise. He had finally been fed and had his flesh wound inspected. It was raw and angry, somewhat like the lawman, but it did not appear to be festering.

The minute that the work party returned, Joe intended that they should depart. The break in the telegraph line would also likely have been discovered, which was something that he certainly could not admit to, so a second bit of sabotage would probably be necessary once they got moving. Whilst the work was progressing, the two detectives inspected their haul of weapons. The awesome firepower of the LeMat revolver impressed Joe. He had relieved Slattery's corpse of the necessary reloads and now carried the weapon tucked into his belt. The other surplus guns were stashed at the rear of the cab.

Finally, with the return of the handcar, the much-delayed supply train could set off to its ultimate destination. With a full load of wood and water, they only had one stop to make before reaching the railhead. As expected, the railroad crew had reported a break in the telegraph line. In their opinion it was the work of disaffected Indians. Once out on the empty plains of Nebraska and well beyond the repaired track, Joe again ruptured the vital line. After that, there was really nothing to do but wait as the Iron Horse effortlessly ate up the miles.

*

Calum Post was both hot and puzzled. The diminutive
New Yorker was in the stiflingly hot canvas tent that con-
stituted his office. He had been checking his telegraph
equipment every hour on the hour. He was young, effi-
cient and proud of his ability. It was those qualities that
had brought him out West to further his career with the
Pacific Telegraph Company. A short while earlier, he had
suddenly found that he was able to transmit a message to
the operator in Columbus. He had rapidly sent an inquiry
as to the whereabouts of the overdue supply train. Then,
before a reply could come through, the line had mysteri-
ously gone dead again. It was all decidedly odd. He knew
that he would have to inform Colonel Cartwright immediately.

Calum had tried many times to rationalize his associa-
tion with the track boss. His services included passing on
the contents of *every* message sent and received at the railhead, and of course keeping to himself every part of
Cartwright's nefarious activities. He told himself that it was
purely a business arrangement and that he wasn't really
doing any harm, but in his more lucid moments he knew
damned well that what he was doing was criminally wrong.
He was a willing party to murder and sabotage. The
problem was that he couldn't now break free of that man's
clutches. He forever lusted after the better things in life
and the money also came in useful to fund his relentless
appetite for whores. And yet, he now seemed to spend
most of his time living in fear of discovery *and* of the track
boss himself.

Gratefully escaping the sweltering tent, Calum made his
way towards the hastily erected barricade. As though

mocking the heat, Cartwright's bear-like physique was enclosed by a black frock coat. An unlit cigar was clamped between his powerful jaws. The operator hated to admit it, but the big man really frightened him. The colonel was staring fixedly back down the track, as though using sheer willpower to hasten the approach of the train. Calum coughed twice before he gained the other's attention. As he related his news, a strange gleam came into the colonel's eyes. At no time did that man say anything. He just nodded repeatedly, all the time watching the young man intently. Calum could feel the beads of sweat forming on his forehead that were only partly due to the summer heat. Finally, a dismissive wave ended his acute discomfort and the track boss turned back to the barricade.

Calum decided, as he beat a hasty retreat, that whatever was coming down that track couldn't be any more intimidating than Thomas Cartwright.

Unlike on the previous day, the train ride was completely uneventful. Mile after mile passed by without the passengers sighting a single human being. What they did see was a huge herd of buffalo on the south side of the Platte. There were so many beasts that the distant terrain turned black. They were literally meat on the hoof for all the tribes of mounted Indians. So long as such numbers remained, no one could conceivably go hungry in any of the territories covering the plains.

As time drifted by, the rhythmical movement of the locomotive gradually lulled Joe into a false sense of security. He was the only one of the three without any tasks to fulfil. So, after a period of such relative tranquillity, it came as a jolting shock when the railhead suddenly swam into view through the lenses of his spyglass. The harsh reality of their situation had returned. He bellowed at Barnaby to reduce speed, and so allow him time to study the situation. With so much smoke billowing out of the stack, their presence had to have been known for some time.

'Well, what do you see?' Bill demanded. With the fireman's job having fallen to him, he was otherwise occupied.

'Looks like it's going to get lively,' Joe responded. 'There's a barricade with rifles behind it, and … and a section of track missing in front of it. Christ, this railway's never going to get finished. Seems like there's more rails lifted than laid!'

As the train slowed down, Bill looked for himself. 'That message to Cartwright sure stirred up a hornets' nest. What's more, he's the only one could have ordered something like that. Which means he must be your man. Well done, *Mister* Wakefield!'

All of a sudden everything seemed so clear, but not to everybody.

'What the hell are you two fellers muttering about?' Barnaby demanded with an air of exasperation. 'Why don't we just head on in there? You've been trying to get to the railhead for long enough.'

Despite the circumstances a broad grin spread across Joe's features as he replied, 'And so we shall, Mister Jones. So we shall. But first you're going to uncouple the front car. That battering ram's going to have to get us into camp.'

As the tell-tale plumes of smoke appeared on the horizon, Cartwright was galvanized into action. 'Shaughnessey,' he yelled. 'Have your men stand to.'

Without waiting for a response, he then strode over to the small horse herd to saddle his mount. The contents of the approaching train were an unknown quantity and the war years had taught him that it was always advisable to prepare an escape route.

For the tracklayers it felt like being back in the army, as they fell in behind the barricade with their deadly muzzle-loading rifles. This time they had no idea who the enemy was, but at least they gained a respite from the backbreaking toil. Their 'long guns' were a mixture of Springfields manufactured in America and Enfields purchased from the British. Both fired the Minié Ball, which, because of its particular construction, could cause horrific injuries to those that it struck.

As the train drew nearer, the Irish walking boss viewed it with disquiet. Surely they were not going to open fire on that? Then he noticed that its advance had slowed. It continued like that for some moments, before coming to a complete stop about a mile away. Squinting against the bright sunlight, Shaughnessey watched as a tiny figure dropped down from the cab and hurriedly made his way to the front of the engine. He was then lost from sight, because for some very odd reason there was a fully laden flat car where you would have least expected it.

'You're plumb crazy. It'd cost me my job and then some to do that!'

Barnaby had reluctantly uncoupled the flat car, but to then be told to ram it into the barricade was just too much. 'That might not be anything to do with us,' he continued incredulously. 'The camp might be under attack from those damned Pawnees.'

Joe regarded him pityingly. 'Those poor dumb sons of

126

bitches gave up the war trail years ago. Besides, this is Sioux territory and they wouldn't be likely to just attack from the north-east down the track, now would they? Christ, a blind man on a galloping horse could see that that barrier is for us alone. The man behind the train-wrecking is over there and he's out to stop us getting Marshal Pritchett into camp. Now get this poxy train moving!'

The engineer had no idea what the lawman had to do with anything, but he was proud of his machine and resented such language. 'There's no call for that kind of talk. You've brought nothing but trouble down on me.'

Bill had heard plenty. 'Enough of this shit! But for us, this train would be smashed to blazes and Slattery would have paroled you to Jesus. We're all that's kept you alive and you damn well know it. Now do as the man says, before I forget that we need you.' With that he ostentatiously rested his right hand on the smooth butt of a Colt Navy.

Barnaby could recognize a threat when he saw one. Choking off any further words, he turned back to his controls and got the locomotive moving again. The other two men exchanged glances and Bill favoured his companion with a knowing smile.

Gradually their speed built up. There was not long to go. The barricade drew nearer and suddenly a warning shot was fired. Barnaby threw them a fleeting look but remained silent. Joe was carefully gauging the distance. Abruptly, his good hand smacked down on the engineer's back.

'Now, hit the brakes!'

With a tremendous screeching of metal on metal, the train began to slow down. Or at least most of it did. Freed from any restraint, the flat car continued relentlessly on its way. As it got nearer, it projected an aura of massive and unstoppable force. With only the one section of track lifted, it was obvious that it would pile directly into the barricade.

With the colonel otherwise occupied, it fell to Shaughnessey to fire the warning shot. The single discharge from his Spencer achieved nothing. The train continued its inexorable advance and the men were getting nervous. A charge by flesh and blood was one thing, but how could any man stand against the Iron Horse? Then the unthinkable happened. Accompanied by the screeching of brakes, the locomotive began to slow down. Yet the flat car, piled high with rails and now partially obscuring the locomotive behind it, continued on its way. It was then that the Irish walking boss finally accepted that Cartwright must have been telling the truth. The train had to have been taken over by assassins and wreckers. Swiftly, he instructed his men to move out on to their flanks. With the vast majority being former soldiers, they knew what was expected of them.

'Aim for the cab, boys. Fire when ready,' their leader bellowed.

A ragged volley rattled out from behind and around the barrier of crossties. The whole front was momentarily obscured by a voluminous cloud of smoke. The engine had slowed to a walk, whilst the unstoppable flat car was almost upon them.

Joe observed the line of rifles descending to the horizontal. It was obvious what was coming next. 'Drop down for your lives!' he screamed out.

Mere seconds afterwards there was a fragmented blast of musketry, as scores of weapons discharged in front of them. The barrage of soft lead balls crashed into every part of the locomotive and even some of the rails on the car behind. Metal striking metal produced a series of tremendous clanging noises, but it was in the wooden cab where the real danger existed. Jagged splinters flew about them and Barnaby suddenly howled out in pain. A sliver of wood had pierced the flesh just below his right eye. Joe witnessed the painful wound, but just couldn't spare the time to help. The flat car was about to strike the barricade, which would provide him with a very small window of opportunity.

'Help him, Bill,' he shouted as he dropped down out of the cab. 'I'm going to get Pritchett before they're reloaded.'

'Run for your lives, boys!' Shaughnessey hollered out unnecessarily. Just before he turned away to flee, he caught a momentary glimpse of a man jumping down out of the locomotive. With his life in danger, he had no time to ponder the meaning of that action. His men scattered like sheep just as the huge projectile left the track. Momentum kept it moving over the wooden crossties until the whole thing smashed into the barricade. No sharp-shooting was required to shatter the chains this time. They could not resist the huge forces suddenly exerted on them. With a deafening din, the whole cargo of thirty-foot-long rails hurtled off the flat car and cascaded on to the ground behind the ruptured fortification. It was then that the first fatality occurred. One man was just too slow on his feet. The end of an iron rail struck him squarely in the back and literally ploughed him into the earth. He didn't even have time to cry out.

Joe Wakefield raced like a man possessed down the length of the train to the passenger car. He was aided in this by the fact that the engine had not yet completely stopped. Reaching his destination, he bounded up the steps and burst through the door.

'What in tarnation's going on?' boomed Pritchett belligerently. He was sour and angry after a long night's captivity. 'Who's doing all that goddamned shooting?'

Without bothering to respond, Joe unsheathed his skinning knife. Alarm momentarily spread over the other man's features. 'Just what're you fixing to do with that toothpick?'

Still maintaining his silence, his captor sliced through the rope that bound Pritchett's legs. Dragging the lawman to his feet, Joe favoured him with a cold smile. By a quirk of fate, that gesture coincided exactly with the rogue rail car striking the barricade and shedding its load. Even at that distance the din was frightful.

'What the hell was that?' Pritchett inquired desperately.

'It's time for you to make good,' Joe responded cryptically. Then he shoved him none too gently to the nearest exit. Pritchett hobbled along painfully, as the circulation only gradually returned to his legs. His hands remained securely tied behind his back. Coming out on to the open-air platform, they were shielded from the railhead by the laden flat cars. With great deliberation, Joe eased the LeMat revolver from his belt. Retracting the hammer, he then flicked the lever, so ensuring that the shotgun barrel would detonate first.

Having guided his prisoner down the steps, Joe stationed himself directly behind the man's bulk and placed the upper barrel of the LeMat against the side of his head.

'Now, you bastard,' he remarked with icy resolve. 'Move

down the side of the train towards the camp. One false move and I'll blow your tarnal brains all over God's creation!'

'You've got no call to treat me like this,' the other man whined. It had abruptly dawned on him just how precarious his situation truly was. Yet with his hands tied and a gun to his head, he really had little option other than to comply. At a steady pace, they moved down the length of the train. Ahead of them lay the ruined barricade and beyond that were large numbers of men milling about in confusion. As they finally drew level with the locomotive, Joe glanced up into the cab. Barnaby was sprawled on the floor, apparently in shock. He had both hands clapped to his face and blood was trickling down on to his grubby overalls. Bill Hickok, crouching near the steps, had both Navy Sixes cocked and ready.

'Don't open fire unless all is lost, Bill. Our only chance is to talk this through, savvy?'

'Yeah, yeah,' came the laconic response.

Joe supposed that that would have to do and so pushed Pritchett forward again.

The rest of the workforce had thankfully got clear. The danger from the inert cargo had swiftly passed, mainly because of the inflexible shape of the rails. Once they had crashed into the ground they simply lay there. Thomas Cartwright, who had remained well clear of the danger area, was quick to realize this.

'Back to your posts, men,' he commanded, without even wasting a glance on the dead tracklayer. 'Reload your weapons and return to your positions.'

It was Shaughnessey who first spotted the new development. 'Mary mother of God, what's after happening now?'

Those fraught words had the men nearest to him turning back towards the train and not all of them had empty rifles.

Locked in a grim embrace, the two men advanced beyond the engine. They really were on their own, as Joe just did not know whom, if anybody, he could trust at the railhead.

There was a loud report and a ball kicked up the ground near their feet. It was too much for the totally exposed lawman. 'You poxy madman,' he bawled out. 'You'll get us both kilt!'

He began to struggle violently, until Joe was forced to bring his left knee up hard into Pritchett's ribs. Even as he did so, there was a sound like a bee in flight next to his right ear. Surely the next ball would have to strike one of them!

CHAPTER FOURTEEN

Shaughnessey shook his head in total bewilderment. Although one of his men was dead as the result of a deliberate collision, nobody had yet fired a shot at them. There were just two fools in a 'lovers' knot' advancing on the camp. In spite of the apparent danger, something about the whole situation was all wrong. After the second wild shot, he made up his mind.

'Stop shooting, all of you. Fire only on my command.' He then advanced a couple of paces and pointed directly at the approaching duo. 'Stand off and identify yourselves.'

There was a slight pause as the man who had remained hidden lowered his revolver. The walking boss noted that it was a LeMat and wondered briefly whether its owner might possibly be a disaffected Confederate officer out to cause some mayhem. Then, amazingly, Josiah Wakefield stepped out from behind the other man.

'Hello, Mike,' he remarked calmly. 'You'd be doing me a great service if you'd have your men lower their weapons.'

133

*

Thomas Cartwright had deliberately hung back to wait on events. He had earnestly hoped that Shaughnessey would order another fusillade, but the fool had suddenly gone soft on him. Biting down hard on his cigar, he strode purposefully into the midst of his men.

'Those two plug-uglies are responsible for wrecking our supply trains. They aim to close us down and see you all out of work. Gun them down like the mangy scoundrels that they are!'

His emotive words drew angry cries from the assembled workforce and many men cocked their weapons. The perceived injustice of it all was just too much for Deke Pritchett. 'You stinking son of a whore, Cartwright. I'll not die for you or any other man.' Spittle flew from his lips as he glared at the armed men around him. 'Yes, I organized the wrecking *and* the killings, but on his say-so and using his spondulix. It's him you need to be pointing those long irons at. Some goddamned speculators back East are paying him plenty to shaft this operation.'

Shaughnessey's eyes widened in shock and dismay. How could this be? Thomas Cartwright was an officer and supposedly a gentleman. He appeared to live and breathe for the Union Pacific.

At that moment the 'officer and gentleman' was seething with frustrated anger and possibly the beginnings of despair. He had never expected such a turn of events. Yet he hadn't given up just yet. 'They hope to trick you with words,' he boomed out. 'Look at your dead comrade. There is no end to their devilry. I am ordering you all to shoot them where they stand!'

That was just too much for the walking boss. Stepping

out between his men and the two newcomers, he raised his hands for all to see. 'Hold fast. There is more to this than meets the eye.' Glancing back, he demanded, 'What say you to all this, Joe?'

Joe Wakefield released his grasp on Marshal Pritchett and with a flourish pulled out his letter of authorization appointing him as a railroad detective. 'Some of you men will know me as a hunter and former soldier. This letter is addressed to me from Lieutenant Colonel Thomas Cartwright, representing the Union Pacific Railroad. It instructs me to use all means necessary to catch the desperados behind the wreckings and killings on said railroad. Well, I've done just that and the trail has brought me right back to *your* track boss. Why else would I place myself in such peril only to spread a canard?'

Joe's plain-spoken words were the tipping point in the confrontation. They seemed sufficiently genuine and honest to at least sow seeds of doubt in the minds of those listening. And they certainly proved too much to take for the man that he had accused. From beneath his sombre frock coat, Cartwright produced a Colt Army and aimed it directly at Deke Pritchett. He had retained sufficient presence of mind to know that that individual was the only man who could actually testify against him in a federal court of law.

Such action took everyone by surprise except Joe, because he was already convinced of the colonel's guilt. Instinctively, he kicked Pritchett's feet out from under him and in doing so saved that man's life. The deadly lead ball flew through the air mere inches above his head. In response, Joe fired the only weapon immediately available to him. With a roar the shotgun barrel of his LeMat discharged in Cartwright's direction.

135

Although his view was obscured, Joe knew intuitively that his prey had escaped serious harm. The short barrel, coupled with the distance between them, meant that a lethal strike was unlikely, and so it proved. The colonel lost his right ear lobe and suffered painful lacerations to his bearded face. They were bloody and disfiguring, but completely failed to bring him down. Realizing that the tide had turned, he then did the only thing left to a man like him. He determined to escape, to fight another day.

Turning on his heel, he sprinted off towards the corral, where a saddled and provisioned horse awaited him. Military discipline is a hard thing to shake off and the workforce was still bemused by his sudden downfall, so no man made any attempt to stop him. Sliding the long poles out of their mountings, Cartwright entered the enclosure, heaved himself up into the saddle and took flight. As he galloped off, flecks of blood flew off his various wounds.

'Shouldn't be a hard man to track,' remarked Bill Hickok, suddenly appearing at Joe's side. 'Not with all that blood dripping off of him.'

Mike Shaughnessey stared hard at the newcomer, before turning to address Joe. 'You won't need to track him at all. I know exactly where he'll be headed. Just you be following the grading west.' He momentarily switched his attention to Pritchett's prone figure as he continued. 'Because of this bastard, the track-laying's fallen well behind, so the graders are camped miles away. Cartwright will likely use his position to poison them against you.'

Joe's face was a grim mask of determination. 'Dan Sturgis had his throat slit because of that cockchafer. His actions here have proven his guilt beyond all doubt. I don't care what's waiting for me out there.' Turning to face Bill, he posed the question, 'Are you with me?'

That man displayed genuine hurt. 'That's a hell of a thing to ask.'

Joe favoured him with a broad smile. 'Very well, then. Let's get to it.'

With that he placed himself squarely in Shaughnessey's hands. 'We can't finish this without you. We need the best horses available, food and water and a couple of oilskin capes in case the weather should turn. This could take a while.'

'You can have whatever we've got,' the walking boss responded eagerly. 'That asswipe lied to us all. He's left a good many widows and orphans too, I'll be bound.'

In a vain attempt to lighten the mood, Bill Hickok had the last word. Gazing around at the idle men and the devastated barricade, he remarked, 'Well, at least these fellers have some work to do. You've finally got a supply of rails!'

Thomas Cartwright was almost overwhelmed by a combination of pain, rage and self-pity. As he spurred his horse away from the railhead, the sheer magnitude of what had just befallen him sank in. All his plans were in tatters and he was reduced to being merely a common fugitive. His mutilated ear hurt abominably and he seemed to be literally covered in blood. His hands were so greasy with it that he could barely grip the reins. There seemed to be no possible way out of such an appalling situation. But then inevitably his sharp mind got to working and logical thought gradually began to assert itself.

Getting a grip on his overheated emotions, Cartwright slowed down to a walk and studied the ground behind him. His back trail was deserted, so there was no point in needlessly thrashing his mount. That persistent bastard Wakefield would doubtless come after him, but it would take him a while to get his possibles together. All the track boss had to do, for that was still his official title, was reach the graders' camp to gain sanctuary. There was no tele-graph link between the two sites, so if he told them that he was being pursued by road agents or the like, the workmen would have no option other than to protect him. But what to do then?

He couldn't remain in the camp for long, because word was bound to circulate as to the true state of affairs. No, he would have to wait until dark and then make a break for it. Keep heading west. Far west! Oregon or possibly California was the place for an enterprising man like him. The gold-rush boom days may have petered out for private individuals without capital, but there would be plenty of other opportunities.

'It'll make life a lot easier if this bastard just bleeds to death,' remarked Bill as they trotted along by the side of the graded earth. 'At least we don't need a half-breed tracker to follow up this trail. Even you could manage it,' he joshed lightly.

'I need him alive,' Joe responded with deadly serious-ness. 'I want to drag him before General Dodge in Chicago, to answer for his bad deeds. There's been a lot of bloodshed recently and I need to justify it. God knows, it's hard to live with. I thought the country was supposed to be at peace now.'

Even the normally irrepressible Bill Hickok was affected by his companion's dark and intense mood, so for the remainder of the journey the two men contented them-selves with silent scrutiny of the terrain. The sun was reaching its zenith by the time they sighted the track-graders' camp. With the exception of survey parties, this was the most western point to have been reached by the Union Pacific Railroad.

With the only trees being cottonwoods located to the south by the Platte River, there was no cover of any kind available. Careful study through his spyglass showed Joe that they were expected. Many of the large workforce had downed tools and had rifles at the ready. Under those circumstances, there was no possibility of a quick surprise rush such as was favoured by the Sioux. And yet such grave odds entirely failed to daunt Bill Hickok.

'I'm going to see if those sons of bitches are awake out there,' he announced with gusto.

Joe knew that there was little point in trying to stop him, but he did have one deadly serious instruction. 'No killings! That's all I ask. Those men are under Cartwright's orders because they don't know any different.'

'Yeehah!' hollered Bill by way of acknowledgement. With that, he dug his heels into his horse's flanks and they were away. Man and beast charged towards the encampment. It was almost as though the animal sensed his rider's excitement. The thundering hoofs seem to match the beat of his pounding heart. As the distance narrowed, Bill began to weave his mount from side to side with consummate skill, whilst at the same time carefully scrutinizing the graders' dispositions.

'Goddamn,' he thought. 'There's nothing finer than to be in action!'

It was then that the first shots rang out. They immediately had a sobering effect. Seeing the muzzle flashes with frightening clarity, he abruptly decided that there was nothing else to gain from his suicidal charge. The rifled musket was fearfully accurate and with so many former soldiers drawing a bead on him, someone was bound to get lucky. Tugging on the reins, he urged his horse into a tight turn and an urgent retreat. In a final flamboyant gesture, he removed his wide-brimmed hat and gave the camp's occupants a grandiose wave.

'Are you happy now?' queried Joe acidly.

Bill dropped down from his mount and eyed him belligerently. 'You're all shit and no sugar, Wakefield! Back off before I decide I don't like you any more. We knew they were out there and ready for us, but I wasn't just joy-riding. I actually saw Cartwright. His horse is ground-tethered at the west end of the camp. My guess is that come nightfall, he's going to hightail it out of there and try to put some distance between him and trouble. So you and me will have to be ready for him.' He paused briefly before adding, 'Are you backed up yet?'

'Some,' allowed Joe. Then he managed the ghost of a smile. 'Yeah, yeah. So you did good. Just try not to take a bullet tonight. I've already lost one good friend on this trip.' Which was as close as someone like Josiah Wakefield ever got to demonstrating his affection for another man.

The passage of time always seems to drag when men are waiting on a significant event. As though providing confirmation of this maddening fact, it took an age for the sun to go down. Until then, because of a lack of natural cover, the two railroad detectives had to endure the broiling prairie heat. The experience was only made tolerable by their using the capes as sunshades and drinking plenty of water. They deliberately kept in sight of the encampment and half-expected a sortie of armed track-graders. That one never took place was possibly another benefit of Bill's earlier display.

Finally the great red orb slid below the horizon and the time had come to make a move. Gratefully mounting up, they carefully made their way around the camp so that they were now facing it from the west. The wind blew the sound of voices towards them, but no lights were visible. For that night at least, it was a cold camp. If Cartwright intended slipping out under cover of darkness, then he would have to come through them. And, since only a fool would travel at speed in the gloom, it was likely that he would walk out leading his mount.

The two men ground-tethered their horses well to the rear and then selected separate positions about ten yards apart. They lay down and readied their weapons. Both men knew their business. Any firefight would be at close range and quite possibly messy and confused. Because of the time of year, it would never get truly dark, so the waiting men had the advantage. Joe's worst fear was that the colonel would recruit innocent workmen to accompany him.

With only one hand fit for service, Joe had again picked the LeMat. A shotgun blast to the legs would likely injure rather than kill their prey and did not require pinpoint accuracy. At least, that's how he viewed matters until he heard the sound of approaching footsteps. 'Goddamn it to hell,' he muttered. There were suddenly three of them visible in the gloom; the cunning devil had indeed picked two men of similar build to accompany him.

'Oh shit,' was Bill's reaction. He would have readily shot all three of them, but the choice was not his and so he held his fire. He noted that only one man led a horse, but that bastard Cartwright could easily have delegated that task.

141

*

Joe was in an agony of indecision. Fate had decreed that the men would pass by his position first. If he didn't act soon, they would be upon him. 'Stand fast and drop your weapons,' he commanded. 'We have you covered.' With only the wind for company, his words sounded loud and bold.

He had expected confusion and maybe a little wild shooting, but it was not to be. The colonel had also picked men who knew how to soldier, because the three men abruptly dropped to the ground and lay quite still and silent. The two sides were apparently at a stand-off, but there was one thing that Joe could shoot at. Taking the LeMat in his left hand, he drew his Colt, cocked it inside his jacket and regretfully drew a bead on Cartwright's horse. Even in the dim light its bulk was visible. If nothing else, he could at least leave the son of a bitch afoot.

Closing both eyes, so as to retain his night vision, he squeezed the trigger. As the revolver crashed out, Joe rolled rapidly to his left. He knocked his left hand on the ground and winced with pain. From before him a rifle discharged and a Minié Ball kicked up earth in the exact spot that he had just left. At the same time, the horse screamed in pain and collapsed on to the ground. There it lay whinnying in agony as its lifeblood drained away into the earth. Joe hardened his heart to the beast's pitiful cries and peered into the darkness for any sign of movement. He had no doubt that the marksman had already shifted position.

Then, out of his peripheral vision, he spotted a single shape travelling rapidly to his left. That could only have been Cartwright. Joe desperately wanted to call out a warning to his companion, but knew that it would only forewarn the furtive figure. Instead, trusting to Bill's abilities, he decided that it was time to reel in the other two men. It would involve great risk, but his blood was well and truly up.

Clutching the heavy LeMat, he carefully lowered the hammer on to the percussion cap behind the shotgun barrel. Drawing in a deep breath, he drew his right arm back and hurled the revolver towards where he thought the two graders were skulking. He leapt to his feet while it was still in the air and pounded towards their position. If the cap failed to detonate, then all was very likely lost.

The gun crashed out before he had even covered two paces and the resulting muzzle flash proved the worth of his bold gamble. A few yards away, two workmen with rifles lay on the ground. Caught completely unawares by the sudden shotgun blast, they were turning to face the new threat as Joe came up behind them. Looming over them in the murk, he cocked his Colt.

'Drop those irons, boys,' he grimly commanded. 'You've had your chance.'

Bill Hickok felt rather than saw the shape approach his position. He possessed a sixth sense for trouble and as usual it served him well. As the figure crept closer through the gloom, Cartwright's stocky physique became discernible. Lying flat on the ground, Bill had both his Navy Sixes cocked and ready. He had sensibly ignored the earlier shots, realizing that the only thing in pain was a dumb animal. And now his chance had arrived. His inclination was to gun down the cockchafer without any warning whatsoever, but Joe's earnest request to take him alive surfaced in his mind.

143

'Goddamn it to hell,' he mused. 'Why do I have to work for a man with a conscience?' Then in a loud voice he barked out, 'Freeze!'

As the other man did just that, Bill got to his feet and moved in closer. It indeed proved to be the ruthless and corrupt Colonel Cartwright. Even in the poor light, the bloody lacerations from the earlier confrontation were plainly visible above the line of his facial hair. He held his Colt Army close to his chest and appeared to be contemplating its use.

'I'd just as soon kill you now,' continued Bill conversationally. 'But then we'd have to tote you back to camp and you're no lightweight. So what say you place that piece on the ground, otherwise I'll just have to give you a very painful flesh wound.'

The track boss stared at him long and hard before emitting a big sigh. 'I don't know who the hell you are, saddle-tramp, but you'll pay for this!'

It was at that moment that the LeMat hit the ground and the sixteen-gauge smooth-bore detonated. The loud report and sudden flash of light in the night sky caught Bill's attention for a mere second, but it was enough. Cartwright took his chance and squeezed off a shot. Without the time to take proper aim, he had just pointed at his opponent's torso and luck did the rest. The ball struck Bill in his left side. At such close range the momentum combined with shock was sufficient to knock him sideways and then on to his knees.

Cartwright's inclination was to finish him off, but two things deflected him from that end. The muzzle flash had temporarily robbed him of his sight and then there was another gunshot from off to his left. He was by no means a timid man, but the opportunity to flee into the dark presented itself and he took it. Stumbling away from his victim, he strained to see what lay ahead. It was then that he had another stroke of luck. There before him stood a ground-tethered horse, conveniently saddled and ready to go.

Yanking the picket pin from the ground, the colonel heaved himself aboard and took off into the night. If he had taken the time to look about him, he would have spotted a second animal. By stealing that, he could have effectively ended any immediate pursuit, but it was not to be.

Joe had moved in closer to his prisoners to check them for weapons. As the gunshot sounded out from off to his left, he winced and instinctively glanced that way. One of the two men before him took his chance, grabbed a rifle and attempted to swing it up. Cursing the man's foolishness, Joe instinctively kicked out to deflect the muzzle and then took concerted aim at his opponent's shoulder. The railroad detective was fully aware that the grader was innocently acting for the best and that any wound would effectively render him unemployable, but he couldn't afford to be overwhelmed by the two men.

As the hammer struck the copper cap, he again momentarily closed his eyes. A piercing scream tore through the night as the heavy ball smashed into his victim's shoulder. Having retained his night vision, Joe cocked his revolver and swung it over to cover the other man. It proved to be unnecessary. That individual's eyes were suddenly wide as saucers and all resistance was at an end.

Joe was not yet in the mood for appeasement. The whereabouts and condition of his companion was unknown. 'Get him on his feet,' he commanded harshly.

To the accompaniment of much wailing, the uninjured man complained bitterly, 'But he's hurting bad, mister. He needs a sawbones.'

'And he can have one, but not yet,' was Joe's unyielding response. 'Now get him up or I'll put a ball in you as well!'

Together the three men made their way slowly over to Bill's position, with Joe carefully using his two captives as a shield. They found him all alone, on his knees and obviously in great pain, but he was still able to unleash a tirade on his employer.

'That bastard done broke my short rib. I could have shot him from cover, but you just had to have him alive, didn't you? Well, you get on after him, Joe Wakefield, or I'll be coming after you!'

With that, he pitched forward and lay still.

CHAPTER FIFTEEN

The new day found Josiah Wakefield out on the sun-baked plains. For the first time since embarking on his ill-founded mission, he was totally alone. He had eventually managed to snatch a couple of hours' sleep, that being all that remained of the night after all the comings and goings and fraught explanations. The camp had been roused to fever pitch by the shooting and the workforce did not take kindly to the wounding of one of their own. It had taken all of Joe's persuasive talents to convince their leader that his own version of events was true. It was the inescapable logic surrounding Cartwright's perverse escape route that had finally swung the argument his way. Why on earth would a member of the Union Pacific hierarchy flee to safety away from civilization, unless he knew that he was likely to be arrested on sight?

Thankfully, Bill Hickok seemed likely to survive, unless the dreaded greenrod took hold of him. His torso, having been liberally cleansed with whiskey, had been tightly bound and he was asleep under canvas. Cartwright had absconded on Joe's horse on which, amongst other things, was a Sharps rifle. That fact alone boded ill for the pursuit that Joe now intended. It appeared that he was to finally discover the merits of Dan's new Winchester repeating rifle.

So it was that the lone and somewhat worn-out railroad detective made his way westward across the interminable plains. He was of the opinion that his quarry would most likely travel parallel to the Platte River. The summer heat was intense and rainfall unpredictable. Any white man had to stay close to a source of water. That was probably Cartwright's only weakness and Joe would have to trade on it.

The miles passed without producing any sign of life. Joe constantly scanned the horizon with the spyglass from Bill's saddle-bags, but even that benefit was cancelled out by the fact that Cartwright would have undoubtedly found its twin in the purloined bags on his own mount. And all the time, he was thinking on just what would happen when he eventually overhauled his prey. He desperately wanted him alive, and yet that desire alone was responsible for Bill taking a ball in his ribs. Any wound, however minor, could become deadly if infection took hold. That fact was responsible for a depth of concern that gnawed on him more than he would have cared to admit.

The sun arced across the sky as Joe continued his solitary journey. Not one single human being crossed his path, which suited him well enough as he knew that he might easily have more than just Cartwright to contend with. The coming of the railroad had stirred up the always-belligerent Sioux Indians. They, not unreasonably, considered that the Iron Horse would scare away the buffalo and bring more white settlers into their homeland. Union Pacific surveyors had been put to flight on more than one occasion recently, which was one reason why the workforce always travelled with its war-issue rifles.

The close of the day brought him into the small and seedy settlement of Kearney. Its residents mainly consisted of speculators motivated solely by greed, who were counting the days to the arrival of the railroad. His careful inquiry in the town's single saloon revealed that a heavily bearded and remarkably bloodstained individual had indeed passed through earlier that day. It appeared that Joe was closing the distance between them and that was enough for him. Turning his back on any of the dubious attractions available in Kearney, he moved on into the dusk until he was well out of sight and then settled down to a cold camp. Well aware of the Indian habit of running off unguarded horseflesh, he slept with the reins wrapped around his good hand.

As the first hint of dawn arrived, he breakfasted on beef jerky and water. Then, after checking his weapons and defecating, the manhunter saddled up and continued westward. The new day bore all the hallmarks of the previous one, yet some sixth sense told him that this one would be markedly different.

The sun had reached its zenith and Joe was considering reining in for a brief rest stop when suddenly he heard it. A distant gunshot, followed by another and another, came from the direction in which he was headed. His brain told him that it could be buffalo hunters, but his gut told him different. Reaching for his draw-tube spyglass, he scrutinized the open ground ahead. What he saw made him blink rapidly, as though not quite believing his own eyes.

The man that he so desperately sought was galloping hell for leather directly towards him. Cartwright appeared

149

to be injured and kept snatching glances behind him. It was obvious that he now had more than just Josiah Wakefield on his mind. Then Joe saw the reason for the man's frantic flight. Coming on after him at a tremendous pace was a large band of Lakota Sioux. They were painted for war and smelling blood. Which meant that it wasn't just the colonel alone who was suddenly in deadly peril.

Joe heaved the Winchester out of its scabbard and rapidly considered his choices. Running just wasn't an option, as both horse and rider were well used. Besides, if he did attempt it, the erstwhile track boss would be lost to him forever. The only chance for both of them was for Joe to stand and fight. There was no cover worth a damn, so regrettably he would have to create some.

After taking a final glance through his spyglass, he dismounted and removed both his saddle-bags and saddle. Resting his rifle on the seat, he replaced it with the Colt Army. A knife twisted in the pit of his gut as he drew back the hammer. Somehow the killing of a helpless creature seemed far worse than taking a human life. Sadly, he placed the muzzle gently up against the soft flesh behind his horse's left eye.

'Christ, why's it come to this?' he muttered wretchedly.

Hardening his heart, Joe turned away and squeezed the trigger. With a roar the weapon discharged. Warm blood spattered on the side of his face and the outcome was instantaneous. The animal's legs buckled and it collapsed heavily to the ground. As the mixed smells of burning flesh and sulphur assailed his nostrils, he was now faced with a grim reality. If he happened to survive the coming encounter, he would likely have to walk back to civilization.

The cause of all his troubles was fast approaching, as

were that individual's pursuers, who had noticeably gained on him. Cartwright had obviously spotted his possible saviour, because he was frantically urging his mount to greater efforts. From behind him came the sounds of hellish screams, as the half-naked Lakota redoubled their efforts to catch the wounded white man.

There was no time to reload the empty chamber in the Colt. Not that it mattered. If he couldn't stand off the advancing warriors with his remaining substantial fire-power, then all was lost anyway. Joe heaved his saddle on to the deceased animal and then grabbed the Winchester. He levered a round into the firing chamber and stood ready.

With a tremendous thunder of hoofs, Cartwright was suddenly upon him. He brutally reined in his horse and then, as it juddered to a halt, literally fell from the saddle. Joe had a stark choice of either grabbing the horse's reins or his Sharps rifle from its scabbard. Since he couldn't both fight and stop the animal being run off, he chose the weapon. Released from its rider's demands, the terrified horse fled off to the east at a great rate. It was only then that Joe saw the feathered arrow jutting from Cartwright's broad back. It had penetrated deep. The surrounding coat was soaked with blood.

Despite his fearful injury, the railroad boss could still talk. 'You just don't know when to quit, do you, Wakefield?'

'Shut up and shoot,' snarled Joe as he dropped down next to him. The Sioux were coming full chisel, confident of their overwhelming numbers. Their hideously painted features emphasized a primitive savagery that was totally new to the two beleaguered white men. Even taking into account his war service, Joe had never been confronted with anything like this. His hands began to tremble and he knew that he was in real danger of losing his nerve.

'Come on, you bastards,' he screamed out, desperately trying to steady himself. As usual the onset of action was the best antidote to stretched nerves. Sighting down the twenty-four-inch barrel, Joe aimed at the lead animal and fired off the first shot. The .44-calibre bullet struck flesh and blood and brought down both horse and rider. Levering in another copper rimfire cartridge, he sought out the next target. Confronted with a whole line of riders, there was no shortage. Again and again his rifle crashed out, accompanied by Cartwright's Colt. God, but the lever action was just so smooth!

The Indians were so taken aback by the unremitting stream of lead coming at them that they failed to unleash any arrows. They had expected to swiftly overrun the two white men on their first rush, yet instead they had taken casualties. Three of their valuable horse herd were dead; one warrior had a broken neck and the rest were hightailing it out of range. Against all expectations, Joe had just survived his first encounter with the plains Indians.

Watching them gallop away, he suddenly remembered his reluctant ally. Glancing to his left, his heart jumped with shock at what he saw. Cartwright had slumped to the ground. The Colt had slipped from his fingers. His eyes met Joe's searching gaze.

'Sons of bitches have done for me, Wakefield,' he muttered weakly. 'How'd it all come to this?'

'You brought it all on yourself, you damn fool,' returned Joe coldly. 'Your greed has cost the lives of many a good man.'

Nevertheless, once he had reloaded the Winchester, he crouched beside the injured man to see what could be done. Drawing his knife, he cut away the material around the livid wound. It was indeed a fearsome sight.

'The arrow is barbed,' he commented flatly. 'If I was to pull it out, I'd like as not tear you apart. It'll need cutting out carefully by a sawbones, after he's dosed you with laudanum.'

Their eyes locked. Both men knew where this was heading. Without a horse between them and a Sioux war party about to come down their throats, Cartwright's prospects were grim.

'Best I can do for now is to break the shaft off,' Joe continued. 'It's going to hurt some.'

'Well, get to it, then,' the other man responded gamely. 'Dare say you'll enjoy it.'

Ignoring that, Joe took a two-handed grip on the arrow shaft and snapped it at his first attempt. Blood continued to weep from the wound as Cartwright gave out a howl of agony. That sound was suddenly duplicated many times over, as the Sioux warriors prepared themselves for another charge.

Joe had intended to bandage the wound in an attempt to staunch the flow of blood, but there was just no time. Lying down behind his dead horse, he placed his two revolvers on the ground beside him. With Cartwright effectively out of the fight, their survival now rested solely on him. It came to mind that things were going to get very lively. If the Sioux now knew what they were up against and were still prepared to make another rush, then they obviously had murder on their minds. Yet the trembling that had afflicted him earlier was now completely absent. He pulled the butt of the repeating rifle tightly into his shoulder and calmly waited.

The warriors gave out a tremendous collective howl and urged their mounts forward. It never occurred to Joe to count them. There were more than enough to go round and they were closing on him at a tremendous rate. He held his fire until they were at the two-hundred-yard mark and then squeezed off a shot. With the crashing detonation and the whiff of sulphur, a familiar exhilaration took hold of him. As the first warrior fell from his dying animal, Joe levered and fired with ruthless efficiency. He didn't even notice the pain in his injured left hand as it clutched the forestock. His whole being was totally concentrated on working the Winchester. As a small pile of expended cartridges grew next to him, the Sioux continued to fall.

And then, as the distance dropped to fifty yards, the rifle was suddenly empty. There was no time to reload, so he simply dropped it to the ground and drew his Colt Army. There were five chambers remaining against a dozen or more mounted warriors. Drawing a careful bead, he dropped the hammer. There was a comforting roar and another animal slewed sideways in agony. *Four* chambers remained. Again, cock and fire. His deadly foes were so close now that he was aiming up at the riders. *Three* chambers.

He suddenly realized with terrible certainty that he was not going to stop the charge unless he threw everything at them. Taking the Colt in his aching left hand, he grabbed Slattery's big LeMat from his belt. Blind to everything except the approaching Lakota, Joe cocked and fired the two revolvers alternately. He was wreathed in smoke and almost deaf, but a primeval ferocity seemed to be coursing through his body. When the hammer of the Colt dry-fired, he screamed his defiance and hurled it at the nearest warrior.

Never had they faced an enemy like this. It was the nine chambers in the LeMat that finally broke them. Two warriors on foot came at him with short lances and he

154

dropped them both. Even with a ball in his guts, one of them clawed his way towards Joe until another projectile in the head ultimately finished him.

As the remaining warriors turned and ran, one splendidly muscled individual stood his ground. After falling from his dying horse, he had retained only a hunting knife, but for him it was enough. Screaming out a defiant challenge, the massive warrior spat into the dirt to show his contempt for the solitary white man. With steely determination, Joe cocked and fired.

The dull click horrified him. It signified either a misfire or an empty cylinder. The Indian recognized his appalling dilemma and with a guttural snarl, launched himself forward. Frantically the white man cocked the hammer again and adjusted the lever. As the lethal blade reached out towards him, he raised the revolver and squeezed the trigger.

The sixteen-gauge shotgun charge erupted from the lower barrel and struck the warrior square in the chest. The force of it stopped him in his tracks. As the sulphurous smoke cleared, Joe watched the brave man drop to his knees, his bare torso drenched in blood. Then, dropping the weapon like a hot coal, Joe reached for the Winchester and began to cram rimfires through the loading gate.

The surviving Indians were fleeing, some doubled up, others on foot. With a full magazine once again, he began to fire at them, mainly to keep the pressure on. Instinctively, he felt it unlikely that they would return after such slaughter. But yet, once they were out of effective rifle range the remaining warriors halted and commenced to gesticulate in his direction.

Shaking his head in disbelief, Joe turned to check on

Cartwright's condition. The man was slumped on the ground. A trickle of blood ran from one corner of his mouth into his beard. The once steely eyes were now lifeless. The former track boss was quite dead.

'Sweet Jesus,' snarled Joe. 'All this killing and for what?'

And it still wasn't over! The surviving Indians were milling about in great confusion, but showed no sign of actually leaving. Joe was ill-prepared to withstand a prolonged siege. Something extra was needed to tip the balance in his favour. Something like a display of supreme marksmanship that the Sioux could never hope to emulate.

Reaching for his Sharps rifle, he raised the ladder sight and made the necessary adjustments. As ever, windage and elevation were the important factors in long-range shooting. Finally satisfied, he fully cocked the hammer and lined up on the most docile of the distant targets. Breathing deeply and deliberately, he took his time. One shot was likely all that he would need. He squeezed the first trigger.

Exhaling steadily, he suddenly held it and fired. The resulting wail of anger and despondency arising from the far-off group of Lakota testified to his accuracy. One of their number lay twitching on the ground, whilst blood pumped from the gaping wound in his chest.

Mounted or on foot, they collectively turned away. Without once looking back, the defeated and despondent warriors trudged off across the prairie. The lone white man's medicine had finally proven to be too much for them.

CHAPTER SIXTEEN

Major General Grenville Mellen Dodge peered across his vast desk at the travel-stained young frontiersman seated before him. The tale that he had just listened to had both stunned and amazed him, yet for a variety of reasons the veracity of it could not be denied. Contemplatively stroking his full beard, he fixed his piercing gaze on the Union Pacific's so-called railroad detective and attempted to clarify what he had just heard.

'So this Marshal Pritchett admitted before witnesses that Cartwright was a party to this foul plot, but you didn't get the names of any others involved.'

'That's correct, General,' Joe responded quickly. 'Mike Shaughnessey was there. He heard it, but Cartwright made a break for it before we could get him to talk. The US Marshal has hold of Deke Pritchett, but we're a mite short of witnesses, so I guess it's up to you what happens next.'

Dodge nodded pensively. 'That comes with the job,' he remarked, before turning away to stare silently out of the window. His office had a commanding view over the windswept waters of Lake Michigan. The size of it was commensurate with his title of chief engineer.

As the period of silence lengthened, Joe's thoughts

drifted back over the previous few days. After the departure of the remaining Sioux, he had reloaded all his weapons, emptied Cartwright's pockets of specie, watch and personal effects and then trudged off towards the east. He left behind him the body of his enemy, to bloat and rot in the sun, and the saddle for whoever was fortunate enough to discover it.

Luck turned out to be on his side. Cartwright's horse had bolted out of danger, but soon tired of aimless motion. Joe discovered it drinking its fill from the Platte River and gratefully climbed aboard. From then on events had taken their course at whirlwind speed. Or at least, so it seemed to a simple soldier and hunter. Bypassing Kearney, he again slept under the stars and the following day found him back at the graders' camp anxious for news of Bill Hickok. That man proved to be weak, but very much alive and on the mend.

'It don't look like it wants to infect,' was all he would say about his wound. Lying on a makeshift cot, he had then beamed up at Joe. 'Looks like you did good, Wakefield. Real good. You kept your scalp and left that son of a bitch for the buzzards.'

After a night's rest, Joe was off again back to the railhead. He wanted to make sure that Deke Pritchett was still in custody. That proved to be so, but what he also discovered was a telegraph message from General Dodge demanding his immediate presence in Chicago. Shaughnessey had reported all that he knew and the chief engineer was eager for the rest.

There then followed many hours of travel, first on a returning supply train and then as a passenger on the Chicago, Rock Island and Pacific Railroad. He had had no idea of the reception that would await him. There had been a great many deaths, not all of them easy to justify; and also of course there was the destruction of the engine sheds in Omaha.

Dodge cleared his throat and Joe abruptly snapped out of his reverie. The chief engineer was regarding him solemnly, apparently about to pass judgement.

'Thomas Cartwright's death was a tragic turn, but all things considered, it was probably for the best. It would do the Union Pacific's reputation great harm if his role in this sorry business came out. The fact that he should be slain by those most likely to benefit from his sabotage of the railroad does, I think, possess a certain poetic justice. Marshal Pritchett's silence will be assured by the *lack* of charges to be pressed against him. Should word of it ever come out, he will be the first to suffer.'

Joe caught his breath in shock and anger and only with difficulty remained silent. He had no understanding of what 'poetic justice' meant, but the idea that Pritchett should get off with *only* a flesh wound stuck in his gullet.

Affecting not to notice, the chief engineer continued. 'Mike Shaughnessey's promotion to track boss should ensure his co-operation. As for your part in all this, well, you appear to have displayed great tenacity and resolve. I think that a sizeable cash bounty is in order. It is only a shame that we cannot restore to you the digit that you are now sadly missing.'

Joe instinctively glanced down at his bandaged hand before posing a question. 'And what of the men behind this conspiracy? What will happen to them?'

The response to that was disappointing but unsurprising. 'As is often the way with men of influence, they will get away free and clear. But what about you? What do you wish to do, now that you no longer have a job?'

'I have a friend to see to, back out West, and then I thought I'd find out if the railroad could use another hunter. You've got a big workforce and I could do with a quieter life.'

The railroad boss's features creased into a broad smile and he actually laughed out loud. 'I'm sure if you were to apply to the new track boss, he might could look upon your request favourably. After all, he's got you to thank for creating the vacancy!'

And with that, the interview was over.